All Things New

A Fable of Renewal

By Rodger Price

Published by Reformed Church Press, 475 Riverside Drive, New York, New York 10115.

Dedication

This book is dedicated to pastors: women and men who heard God's call and followed it into our lost and broken world so loved by God—a world filled with people who don't fully understand them and who often do not treat them as they should be treated, which is with respect and encouragement.

Cover Design

Carl Meinke designed the cover for *All Things New*, with inspiration from Ann Saigeon.

Acknowledgements

I consider this book to be a bit of a miracle as it certainly would not have happened without God's promptings and the help and encouragement of many people.

Thank you, Amanda, for your love of thirty-five years and your ongoing encouragement and "coaching."

I also thank Karen Mulder, my very good friend and an author herself, whose encouragement kept me believing that maybe I could write the story that was cooking inside my head.

Many thanks go to Ann Saigeon, who is closer to being my coauthor than my editor. Thank you for your encouragement from the start and for your many ideas that made this story much richer.

I thank my teammates at the Reformed Church in America who worked on this book, especially Ken Eriks, Vicky Menning, Carl Meinke, Barb Koorndyk, and Phil Tanis. I also thank the Lilly Foundation for the Sustaining Pastoral Excellence grant that allows us to do the work we do with pastors.

And finally, and most importantly, I thank God for blessing me with this story. I pray that we have told it in a way that will move people to pursue God more deeply, explore themselves more honestly, and engage their brothers and sisters more lovingly.

Introduction

All Things New explores the importance of deep, meaningful relationships in helping Christian leaders grow and become more fulfilled and effective in all areas of their lives, including their ministries.

Rodger Price wrote *All Things New* as a creative way to introduce pastors to the benefits of belonging to a network—a small group of five to seven pastors who covenant to meet regularly for fellowship, accountability, and spiritual renewal. While no real people are depicted in the book, its characters and events reflect Rodger's experience with and knowledge of pastors networks.

Rodger serves the Reformed Church in America, where he and his peers work to revitalize congregations by helping church leaders experience spiritual renewal. In that capacity he has helped implement a process whereby RCA pastors who meet in networks can be revitalized by discovering or rediscovering their reason for being, their values, and their vision for the future. RCA pastors know that process as Purposeful Living. In *All Things New* the process is called Living by Design.

Living by Design, the process the pastors in *All Things New* use to formulate their personal calling statements, is modeled on the Focused Living process, which was created by an organization called Christian Resource Ministries (CRM). CRM began offering Focused Living retreats for church leaders in the 1990s. Purposeful Living/Living by Design has also been shaped by the recent pastors networks movement, which has touched the lives of hundreds of pastors.

Copies of *All Things New* are available at cost through Faith Alive Christian Resources (1-800-333-8300 or www.FaithAliveResources.org). The book is also available free as a downloadable PDF file on the Reformed Church in America website: www.all-things-new.org.

Table of Contents

Chapter

Questions to spark discussions about the material in each chapter are available online: www.all-things-new.org.

Chapter One

The World Is Flat and So Is Life

The email subject line caught Cal's eye: "Free Lunch." He sighed.

The message was from Tony.

Cal felt a twinge of guilt for thinking of Tony, another pastor in the community, as a competitor. But part of Cal argued: "In this small town you need to keep an eye on what other pastors are doing in their ministries."

One thing he knew for sure: he would never share with anyone how he really felt about his cross-town rival.

It was another Monday morning. The kids had left for school. Pam had already left for the church office. The house was quiet. Snowflakes drifted down beyond the window. Cal poured a second cup of coffee and sat to finish going through his email before heading to the office himself.

"No such thing as a free lunch," he grumbled. He punched "Open" to read Tony's email. It began:

> I recently read a book where the author said that most people live in a sort of voluntary prison, wearing a mask that covers up issues they're struggling with inside.

Cal pushed back from the desk a little. He felt like someone was pointing out the mask he wore around Tony. The email continued:

> Those words really hit home for me. I'd like to meet over lunch with you and a few other pastors in the area to talk about it.

The open tone of the email was a surprise. Tony and Cal belonged to the same denomination, but although they had lived close to each other for the last five years, and even though he and Pam had run into Tony and his wife at kids' soccer games and a few social events, they hadn't really gotten to know each other.

Recently Cal had lost more than a few members to Tony's church. The most difficult to lose were two young families. Cal had even wondered if Tony was intentionally targeting some of his younger members to stoke membership numbers for the denominational year-end reports.

He sipped his coffee and read the first line of the email again. Those three words stood out: "wearing a mask."

It was the second time a phrase had caught him off-guard recently. The other was the title of a book he'd spotted on a shelf at the local bookstore: *The World Is Flat.* It had stopped him in his tracks. "*My World Is Flat* could be the title of my autobiography," he had thought. "A pretty dull autobiography. Okay, well, maybe just the last few years. Because it hasn't always been like this."

In fact, when he and Pam had started serving as co-pastors at First Church of Jefferson five years earlier they both had thought they couldn't have scripted life any better than it had turned out. On top of vocations that aligned nicely with their beliefs and natural gifts, they had flexible schedules, three happy, healthy kids, and a nice house on a cul-de-sac with a big backyard. Two years back a couple of contractors in their congregation had built them a jumbo-sized swing set and slide. Theirs was one of the best backyards in town, and lots of neighborhood kids came to play when he and Pam were around.

Jefferson used to be a small town surrounded by fields, with a main street and a local café. Now it was a suburb that had grown by about 30 percent over the past ten years, and people of many ethnic and racial backgrounds had joined the community. Today about 50,000 people called Jefferson home. It was a good place to raise a family, but older citizens were not quite sure how to embrace the changes that were happening.

Unlike the surrounding community, First Church hadn't changed much in a generation. Most of the 150 regular attendees were over 55. They never seemed to think about the problems that could be on the horizon for a church that was out of sync with its community. Cal and Pam had talked about this with each other, but they weren't sure what to do about it. There were enough funerals and marriages to attend to and enough programs to juggle that they just hadn't had much time—or energy—to confront what they referred to privately as "the change thing."

At least that was their excuse. Cal knew it was an excuse, and their unwillingness to raise this important issue was just another example of just how much things really had changed for himself and Pam. Years ago they'd had so much more passion for ministry, and if he was honest, for all of life.

He remembered the excitement of his new faith in Christ when he was seventeen. Then at a gathering in college called Campus Light, a student ministry, he had met Pam. They had started working together finding ways to feed hungry people in a run down area of the city. As they'd grown closer to each other and deeper in their faith, they had found ways to show God's love to people who could be hard to reach.

Cal felt a stab of remorse as he remembered the passion he had experienced back then—for both Pam and the ministry. Where had that passion gone? How had life gone so flat?

He wandered into the family room and stared at the wedding photo they still displayed on the piano. He and Pam had married thirteen years ago, right after college. Then Cal had entered seminary and Pam had taken a job in banking. They'd had their first child, Justin, when Cal was in his final year of seminary.

Wow. That had been eleven years ago.

After Cal had graduated from seminary, he'd served three-quarters-time as associate pastor at a large church in Illinois. Pam had gone back to work at the bank part-time. Cal had given her his wholehearted support when she decided she too would attend seminary.

Cal smiled. Juggling his ministry, her job, her schooling, and a toddler had been a real challenge for them. And before Pam completed seminary, the girls had come along, Jessica and then Jordan.

He remembered Pam's graduation as quite a celebration. Now he and Pam would leave behind the craziness of her job and full-time studies. They would have time for each other. They would finally be able move into the kind of life they had always envisioned together.

And yes, the life they had built together was good in so many ways. So where did the passion and excitement go? Even his marriage had become flat. It wasn't a bad marriage, but it wasn't alive with passion either. He knew it was partly because he and Pam were both very busy serving First, and she did more than her fair share with parenting and running a smooth household.

Things hadn't turned out the way he had expected. Cal had hoped to share everything with Pam. Everything about life and work and ministry. But lately he found himself holding back. Not worrying her with every detail. Protecting her from information she might find troubling. He told himself it was an act of love, but he also had to admit that he often felt lonely. Maybe flatness was just part of life as a responsible pastor and father and neighbor. Maybe everyone felt like this.

In a flash of self-awareness, Cal had to admit that his ministry was flat too—not bad, but not alive like he had thought it would be at this stage. The great majority of people attending First had good hearts, he thought, but something was missing. It felt like they were just going through the motions...just existing...just getting by. He often felt he was spending more time managing than ministering. "Herding cats," as he and Pam liked to say when things were especially crazy.

Cal wondered if it was partly because his own personal time with God was flat. He engaged the Bible most weeks when he prepared sermons, but he had to admit that lately that felt more like his job than one-on-one time with the God who had captured his heart seventeen years ago. When he did discipline himself to engage the Bible just for his own growth, he usually found it difficult and forced. Just something else to feel guilty about.

Cal sat back down at the computer, still lost in memories. He recalled how he used to get a thrill from hiking in the woods, fishing a nearby lake, and riding local bike trails. But somewhere along the way, as he took on seminary studies, added kids into the mix, and became a pastor while supporting Pam in her studies, he had stopped doing those things. Now with all the other really important things to do in his life, like preaching, studying, parenting, being a good husband, taking care of the house, pastoral visits to members of the aging congregation, and presiding at all-too-frequent funerals, Cal found himself with no time for hiking, biking, and fishing. "And I have the body to prove it," he thought.

A rush of wind tapped branch tips against the window, snapping Cal back to the present. He stared at the computer screen. The email. It was downright painful to think about attending something that Tony would be hosting. He wondered what good excuse he could come up with.

On the other hand, Tony had admitted that he might be living behind a mask too. Maybe he and Tony had something in common after all.

"What do I have to lose?" thought Cal. Besides, it was a free lunch.

He hit the reply icon and typed:

Just let me know when and where.

Chapter Two

Opportunity Knocks

Cal had been busy over the two weeks leading up to the lunch date with Tony. He hadn't had much time to think about what "sales pitch" Tony might have in mind. Now, driving to the meeting, he realized he hadn't even talked about it with Pam. It seemed like more and more their busy schedules kept them on separate tracks.

When he pulled into a parking space at Third Church, Cal was running late, but he sat in the car for a few moments. His calendar was already full. Did he really have time for another meeting?

A stiff wind blew pellets of ice and snow into his face as he left the warm car and started across the parking lot. It was pretty full for a weekday morning. Cal recalled reading in the local paper about the church's community programs—a preschool, hot lunches for seniors, Alpha and AA classes. He figured that those programs explained why so many people had come out in this bitter cold.

Sure enough, the building echoed with conversations, and the aroma of food cooking filled the hallways. Cal spotted Tony and walked over to say hello. Tony was making introductions among the five other pastors who had come, four men and one woman. "Cal, welcome." Tony smiled, shook his hand, and introduced him to the others. "I think they're ready with lunch for us," he said, leading the group down the hall to a meeting room.

The food was good and the conversation enjoyable as the pastors got to know each other. Cal relaxed a bit.

As the plates were being cleared, Tony stood. "Thanks for taking time to be here today. I'd like to tell you why I've invited you to meet.

"Do you ever feel like you have to wear a mask to hide what you are really feeling inside?"

Tony had Cal's full attention. All of the pastors listened closely as Tony continued.

"That's how I've been feeling for some time. And I have to tell you, it's taken a toll. I realize that, from the outside, people tend to view me as a 'success' as a pastor. And it's true that we have a big new building, lots of programs, a healthy budget. But on the inside, I've felt like anything but a success. I've felt alone. I've felt empty. At times I've felt like a big phony."

This was "wonder boy" Tony speaking? Cal could hardly believe what he was hearing.

Tony held up a book. Cal read the title: *Through Seasons of the Heart*.

"In the email invitation I sent you a couple of weeks ago, I summarized some of the teachings of this book's author, John Powell. I mentioned that he believes most people live in a voluntary prison and wear masks that cover their true condition inside.

"When I read that, I realized that Powell was describing me. I also realized that I wanted more than anything to walk out of my prison.

"I think Powell describes the condition of many people. I remember reading research somewhere that suggested that most people—and especially pastors—feel that they must hide their true selves behind a mask. We fear that if people know what we are really thinking and what we are really like, they will no longer respect us. They may no longer even like us!"

Tony smiled broadly. "I need help. I need a pastor!" he exclaimed, throwing up his hands. The tension that had been building receded a bit as everyone laughed.

"But seriously. I need a place to worship and be renewed, just like the people in my congregation.

"Where does each of you go to worship?

"I'd like us to consider what it might be like for us to worship together as a small group of pastors—a pastors network. It's not my own idea. After reading Powell, I came across an article about pastors networks in one of the magazines I get. The idea of a handful of pastors covenanting to support and encourage each other and hold each other accountable wouldn't let go of me. It seemed like it might be a way to take off my mask, to be myself with people who would understand me.

"I decided to learn more about pastors networks and eventually got some training on how to start one. I've become even more convinced that starting a network is a way to help pastors break out of the prison that Powell describes. That's why I invited you to lunch today."

Cal looked around the table to gauge people's reactions. Two of the men and the one woman in the group sat forward with expressions of interest. Another man wore a noncommittal expression. Yet another looked ready to lose his lunch.

Cal was gripped by a sensation he hadn't experienced in quite a while—a kind of butterfly-in-the gut feeling of excitement and anticipation. Could God be leading him to a place where he could experience real worship again, instead of just leading worship as part of his "job"? Could this be a key to leaving Flat World?

Tony's voice drew Cal's attention back to the room. "Let me read you a passage from *Through Seasons of the Heart*:

> While it may seem to be a safer life behind these facades, it is also a lonely life. We cease to be authentic, and as persons we starve to death. The deepest sadness of the mask is, however, that we have cut ourselves off from all genuine and authentic contact with the real world and with other human beings who hold our potential maturity and fulfillment in their hands.

"And another passage:

> I can understand myself only after I have communicated myself adequately to another. As a result of this growth in self-understanding I will find my patterns of immaturity changing into patterns of maturity. I will gradually change!

"We are taught in Ephesians 4 'to grow up in every way into him who is the head, into Christ.' I'm convinced that to continue to grow and be nourished spiritually, we need a place where we can take off our masks, be our genuine selves with each other. A place to share joys and sadness, to pray for and with each other, and to worship together.

"It's a journey I'm ready to sign up for, and I hope you are too. I'm convinced that the healing and encouragement that will flow from our network will bring us, and our ministries, more alive. I hope it will be a place to engage in real, loving relationships with brothers and a sister who are all in the same boat. Scary challenges face most pastors every day! We need each other."

Tony paused, looking a little sheepish. "I've been going on a bit. Does any of this make sense?"

Everyone either nodded or said yes.

Tony began to describe what the network would look like and gave everyone a handout titled "The Basics of a Pastors Network." He went over the main points on the handout.

"We'll hold monthly gatherings for worship, prayer, breaking bread, sharing what's going on in each others' lives. These meetings will be times of intentional learning and developmental challenge.

"Initially the group will start with a process designed to help each of you clarify your understanding of why God created you; the unique beliefs, values, and passions that God has been creating in you; and what God might be calling you to be—and do—in the coming years.

"The members of the group will challenge each other to be real and to love each other just as Christ loves us...even if it's painful.

"Each pastor's executive committee, or whatever governing body his or her church has, will need to know and support the decision to participate in the network. They must not only support the amount of time that will be necessary but also provide encouragement for inner growth, which might have repercussions for the congregation.

"And finally, each participant will be offered a personal coach, a person who will come alongside him or her to help explore and harvest the wisdom that lies within, along with the Holy Spirit's promptings.

"Now I'd like us to spend a half-hour or so talking about what it would mean for us to form a pastors network."

The room buzzed as everyone joined in the discussion. The conversation continued for at least twenty minutes and could have gone on a lot longer, but Tony stood to call the gathering to a close.

"I'm so glad you all came today. We've covered a lot of information in a very short time, and it's fantastic to see your enthusiasm for starting a network.

"I'd like to propose that we form a network and try it out for six months. I'd also like to give you two weeks to think and pray about whether you want to be a part of this. Talk to people whose opinions you trust to find out what they think about it. And please, if you have questions or just want to talk more about it, don't hesitate to get in touch.

"In two weeks, I'll get a hold of you to find out what you've decided to do. I won't think any less of you if you decide not to join the network, but I sure hope and pray that all of you will."

Cal looked at his watch. Almost three o'clock! He thanked Tony for asking him to come and said quick goodbyes to the others. He hoped he didn't seem rude, but he had an appointment to meet with Justin's teacher at the middle school.

Driving across town Cal struggled with what it would mean to join the pastors network. On one hand, it made perfect sense that pastors needed a place to be themselves, to be encouraged, and to grow spiritually. In fact, it seemed like a cup of cold water extended to his parched soul.

At the same time he resented that this opportunity had come from Tony—especially Tony! Once again Tony would be the one leading the cool new thing in town.

All of Cal's self-doubts came crashing in. He hated to admit that he might not have it all together, even with all of his education, study, prayer, and efforts to do the right thing. He hated that he might be able to preach a great message but couldn't always live it. He felt his insides twist when he thought about God using Tony of all people to reach out to him...and guide him!

That night Cal decided not to bother Pam with all of the turmoil going on inside him. "Tony from Third invited me to be in a group of pastors, and I'm thinking I might do it," was all he said as they got ready for bed.

"Sounds interesting. That's nice of Tony, don't you think?"

Cal just grunted. Pam left it at that. Tony could be a sore topic.

* * * *

Over the next two weeks, Cal wanted to open up to Pam about the network, but he couldn't bring himself to talk about feeling inadequate and full of doubt. He thought about it every day, and prayed for guidance. He was surprised by the strong emotions this idea of a pastors network had stirred up in him.

As promised, two weeks later to the day, Tony called to see if Cal would be open to trying the pastors network for six months.

"I sense that you haven't decided one way or the other about this yet," said Tony after they'd talked for a while. "I want you to know that I really want you to join the group. I'm sure all of us will benefit from knowing you better and learning from you."

Cal could hear Pam's voice in his head warning him that he was too much of a people pleaser. But how could he say no to this guy, even if he didn't really like him?

"Count me in," Cal heard himself say.

As Cal drove up to the house that night he was thinking, "What have I done?" He could sense that the network was bound to change him, which excited and scared him at the same time.

Most of all, he wondered how he was going to be able to handle being around Tony—and experiencing leadership from Tony.

He slammed the car door and stepped toward the front porch. His foot hit a patch of ice and his arms windmilled wildly. His feet flew out and he landed hard on his side and elbow.

Cal lay still for a moment catching his breath, trying not to swear, and testing to see if anything was broken. His mind replayed what his fall must have looked like if a neighbor was watching, and he started to laugh. Oooh, that hurt too.

It was going to be an interesting ride.

Chapter Three

Getting to Know You

"I very much appreciate that you four have chosen to take part in the network. I really look forward to getting to know all of you better."

As Cal listened to Tony open the first pastors network meeting, he felt a twinge of anxiety. The old song "Getting to Know You" popped into his head. If Tony really gets to know what I think, he may not be so glad he asked me to be part of this, thought Cal.

Besides Tony and Cal, the others who had signed on included Juan, pastor of Holy Trinity Church, Curt, pastor of Church of the Savior, and Rex, senior pastor of Jefferson's mega-church, God's Community.

Tony explained that the two other pastors in the original group had let him know that they wouldn't be able to join the network just now because of previous commitments. One of them, Marie, who was associate pastor at New Life Ministries, was especially interested in the network concept, and she and Tony had met to discuss it in detail. Just a few days earlier, she had told him she was looking into getting trained to lead a network especially for female pastors, which he thought was a great idea.

"One of our top priorities in this network needs to be to create a safe environment—a place where we can laugh, be real, and be understood," Tony continued. "And a place to love and be loved by others who understand the unique challenges pastors face.

"Before we enjoy lunch together, let's take a minute to pray.

"Lord, we pause to honor you, to praise you, and to thank you for life. We thank you for this great day and this new beginning—this chance to come together with our brothers to explore what you have before us, as individuals and as a small group of pastors. I thank you that these new friends have chosen to take a chance in walking together in ministry.

"Forgive us, Lord, for the many times that our thoughts, words, or deeds disappoint you. Help us recognize these times and help us change. We want to please you.

"Bless this food we are about to eat, and bless our time together. Use this time to form us, for you are the potter and we are your clay.

"Jesus, we pray all these things in your holy name. Amen."

Over lunch they made small talk about their kids and their ages and schools, about where they had grown up and gone to school themselves. All very pleasant—and flat, thought Cal. He found himself rummaging through his mental to-do list for the rest of the week. This meeting was scheduled to go until five. Suddenly that seemed like an eternity.

Another thought flashed into his consciousness: Maybe it's difficult to be here because Tony is leading—and leading so well. This hardly seemed like the guy who admitted he felt like a phony a few weeks ago. Cal realized Tony was looking right at him. Tony smiled and Cal smiled back.

After lunch Tony read from Psalm 139 and asked everyone to tell in a few sentences what they had heard from the passage and how it might be speaking to them today. Everyone took a turn sharing, and Tony closed their devotions with a short prayer.

Cal had wanted to spend more time unfolding what each of them had found in what the psalmist was saying, but Tony seemed intent on moving on. He spent the next ten minutes talking about his ministry, his struggles, his family, and his divorce ten years earlier—something Cal had never known about. He ended with, "I want to grow even if it kills me."

Tony then invited each of them to share more than they had previously about themselves.

Cal learned that Juan had grown up in Toronto, Curt had been adopted as an infant and had been trying to locate his birth parents, and Rex had been a successful entrepreneur before attending seminary.

When it was Cal's turn, he gave a brief overview of his life and the pastorate he and Pam shared. In a way he felt like he'd let the group down by not sharing something more interesting.

"Thanks everyone," said Tony. "I'd like to move a little deeper, and I want to start by asking you to think about three big questions. Number one: Why did God create you in the first place?; number two: What beliefs, values, and passions has God been forming in you throughout your life?; and number three: What might God be calling you to be and do with the remainder of your life?

"In my network facilitator training, we were introduced to a process that helps people gain clarity in answering these questions. That process is called 'Living by Design.'

"We'll begin this process by constructing timelines of our lives. Start by thinking about all the people, experiences, and situations that have formed who you are today." On a flip chart, Tony wrote: People, Experiences, Situations.

"This will take a significant chunk of our time this afternoon, but even though it's tough to do, the people I know who have taken the time to build this timeline, myself included, have found it to be very meaningful work."

The room fell quiet except for the scratch of pens and paper and the tapping of laptop keys as they set to work. Cal looked up at one point and noticed Rex frowning as he wrote. Curt looked a little misty eyed. Each pastor seemed deeply involved in the task.

They took a short break, and when they returned Tony shared a few key points from his own timeline. He talked about his experience as an all-state athlete in high school and in theater at college. He talked about experiencing a spiritual epiphany during his senior year of college, and how he had given his life to Christ in a single moment and had never questioned that decision.

He also talked about what led his marriage to fail, and that he knew he was largely to blame. It was obvious that it was still hard for him to talk about. He shared how all of these things, good and bad, had affected him when they happened, and how they still affected him.

The group listened intently. Cal was surprised by Tony's willingness to share so honestly about himself. He had to admit that he felt honored to be trusted in this way. This was very different from the way he had experienced pastors behaving around each other. Usually there was an atmosphere of competition—or at least a strong guardedness—and Cal couldn't think of any time that a pastor had admitted any kind of failure.

Cal offered to go next. Before he began, Tony reminded the group about the importance of confidentiality.

Cal surprised himself by his willingness to share personal stories from his past. He talked about his faith journey and how, like Tony's, it had begun with a commitment to Christ when he was a young adult. He choked up a little when he talked about how much the people in his faith community meant to him back in college, and about the indelible impact they'd had on his life.

The others expressed understanding and encouragement, and he opened up even more.

"I've known what it means to have faith that's alive, but I have to tell you, I haven't experienced that aliveness lately. Lately life in general seems flat, and I've been a little concerned about that."

Cal knew he had been feeling more than a little concerned, but he couldn't bring himself to be that open.

"I think this feeling of flatness—this feeling that the spark has gone out of life—has to be affecting my ministry, my wife, my kids. Thinking about that makes me feel guilty, which makes it even worse. My life should be great. I've racked up all the essentials: a good career, a great family, a nice house in the 'burbs. Why am I so unhappy?"

Cal felt uneasy when he thought about not having shared thoughts this deep with his wife or any good friends. Okay, if he was honest, he didn't have any close friends. But Pam—he owed it to her to open up like this.

When Cal was done sharing, he felt like maybe he had shared too much with people he didn't even know. But he also felt a sense of peace that he hadn't touched in quite a while.

It helped when Curt also shared freely about the good and the bad from his timeline, and then Juan, and finally Rex. Cal found that listening to the others' stories seemed almost sacred, and he was amazed at how close he felt to these men after just one short afternoon.

When Rex had finished sharing, Tony thanked each of them again for their willingness to be open with each other.

"That openness is key to the success of a network," he added. "If we decide to form a network, there are four commitments I'd like us to make to each other." He handed each of them a copy of the commitments and began reading them.

"Number one: We promise to play by "Vegas Rules"; like the ad says, 'What Happens Here Stays Here.' It's the same for the network.

"Number two: We will make attendance at the monthly meetings a priority; the value of these meetings comes from the relationships we will be building. We need to be present to build those relationships.

"Number three: We will come to meetings with an open heart and a willingness to be real with each other. This will be a place where you can take off your mask, where you can walk out of your prison and be yourself and be accepted.

"And number four: We will bring a willingness to love each other and to be straightforward with each other, and we will never talk behind each others' backs. It goes without saying that the place where you would be willing to take off your mask has to be a place where it's safe to do that."

In closing Tony gave the group an assignment to complete over the next month. It involved reading Scripture and reflecting on why God had created them. He asked that they be ready to share their insights at the next meeting. Then they chose the date of their next gathering—exactly four weeks away and an hour earlier.

"I'm really looking forward to meeting regularly with this group and walking through the next six months of life together," Tony said. "I know it will be powerful for me, and I hope it will be for each of you too."

At first Cal felt like he was floating on his drive home. What an amazing afternoon! But as he drew closer to 323 Beechtree Court, the guilt about having shared so openly with relative strangers returned. Now here he was going home to flat relationships with his own wife and kids. He felt a deep longing to experience the same openness and closeness with them. He knew this needed to happen. He had no idea how it would happen.

Where would he begin?

Chapter Four

Cal, Meet Cal

After dinner and homework and getting the kids off to bed, Cal and Pam were finally alone.

"Honey, we have to talk," said Cal.

Pam drew her sweater more closely around her and lowered herself into a chair that faced the sofa where he was sitting. "I'm listening."

The events of the afternoon poured out. If Pam was surprised at his enthusiasm about the network, she didn't show it.

He came to the part about the feelings of guilt as he returned home.

"I felt good when I left the meeting, but as I got closer to home I started to feel awful." Pam's eyebrows registered surprise.

"No, no. I mean, I felt guilty because I was so open with people who were practically strangers about things that I hadn't been open with you about, Pam. I'm sorry. I'm really, really sorry…"

When he lifted his face she could see in the dim light that his eyes had filled with tears.

"It has been pretty lonely lately," said Pam. "I miss the man I love." Her eyes filled with tears too.

"I've held a lot of my feelings to myself the past few years," Cal continued. "I didn't want to talk about the disappointment I've felt with life. I was afraid you would think I was disappointed with us. But that's not it. Please believe me. I love you as much as ever."

"What are you disappointed about, Cal?"

"I know I don't have any right to complain," he began. "I mean, how many guys wouldn't want my life? You're everything I want and admire in a woman, the kids are doing great. We have a great life together. But something is missing. It's like so many of the things that were really important to me, to us, have fallen by the wayside."

It was silent for a few moments before Cal continued. "You know, it's funny, but I've been dreaming lately about life back in our college days. We really struggled, but life was so…I don't know, so alive!"

They both grinned. "I miss those times too," said Pam. "But that was then."

"I know, I know. But wouldn't you like to feel like that again? We pastor a church together. We're supposed to show people the joy of Christian living. Instead you're lonely, and I'm flat!"

Pam crossed to him and took his hands in hers. "We got off track for a bit, but we can get it back."

"Are we off track a bit?" he asked. "Or is there more to it than that?"

They hugged and cried and talked about how much they had gradually moved away from a relationship that was fully alive. They remembered how they first met in college, how they worked side by side in ministry together and couldn't wait to be with each other.

"Pam, I know God's going to help us put this back together. I have no idea how or what it will look like, but I'm pretty sure God's at work right now."

The clock on the mantel softly chimed midnight. Pam couldn't resist: "It's a new day!"

"You are hopelessly goofy, you know that," said Cal.

Pam crossed her eyes and stuck out her tongue. She ruffled his hair. "Way past bedtime," she said.

* * * *

The next morning and in the days afterward Cal and Pam found ways to start really connecting again. Sometimes they took long walks together and said very little. They made time to play more with the kids.

Over the next few weeks Cal felt some of his joy and enthusiasm for life coming back. It had happened since the first network meeting, and he was grateful for the part it had played in beginning what he now thought of as his recovery. The first step of a recovery program.

Cal found himself appreciating what Tony had done in reaching out to him, and in providing a way to be more authentic and vulnerable with brothers and sisters in Christ.

The next meeting was still a week away. Cal fired off an email.

> Tony, I just wanted to say thank you for taking the initiative to start our pastors network. I really appreciate that you invited me to be part of it. I have already benefited from the experience and am excited to see how this will impact my life and ministry. Please let me know if there is anything I can do to help with the upcoming meeting.
>
> Blessings,
>
> Cal

Tony wrote back just a few minutes later.

> Cal,
>
> Thank you for this encouragement. It means A LOT to me!
>
> The only thing I would ask you to do in prep for our meeting next week is to pray for our time together. Pray for each of us to experience God and real community.
>
> Pray that our hearts would be open to new revelations about who we are and what God might have in store for each of us.

> At the next meeting I want to talk with you about something I believe God has laid on my heart about you in particular.
>
> God bless you till then. Tony

Me in particular?

What could Tony want to talk about? Cal wondered if Tony could have picked up on his less than charitable thoughts toward him. Pam always said he'd be a disaster in a poker game.

Suddenly Cal wasn't so eager to see Tony again.

* * * *

He was still chewing on the meaning of Tony's email as he walked through the doors of Third for the next pastors network meeting.

"Let's each tell a little about what's been happening in our lives," Tony began once Cal, Juan, Rex, and Curt had taken seats around the table.

"It's hard to put into words, but I've noticed that I feel less stressed," said Juan. "I think hearing about what some of you have been going through has made my own baggage feel a little lighter."

"I can relate to what you're saying, Juan," said Rex. "Even though we've just started this group, I sense that something is changing in me and in my relationships with some of the people I'm closest to."

Curt seemed reluctant to join in, and no one pressed him.

It was clear to Cal that the emotional journey he had been experiencing wasn't unique to him. He had thought of it as a sort of unintended consequence of the first meeting, but after hearing from the others he suspected that it was exactly what was meant to have happened.

Tony held up his well-worn copy of *Through Seasons of the Heart*, the devotional book he'd referred to at their first meeting and that he'd said he'd been immersed in for the past year. He began to read:

> It seems obvious that human communication is the lifeblood and heartbeat of every relationship...A "human loner" is a contradiction in terms. The existence of a human in isolation from others is like a plant trying to survive without sunlight or water. No new growth can occur and the life that does exist begins to wither and will slowly die. For us to be is to be with another or with others. The quality of our human existence is grounded in our relationships.

"And here again is a passage I shared at our first meeting." He turned to another page, and read:

> I can understand myself only after I have communicated myself adequately to another. As a result of this growth in self-understanding I will find my patterns of immaturity changing into patterns of maturity. I will gradually change!

"Friends, I'm convinced that our time together can become, to paraphrase John Powell, a time of communicating ourselves adequately to each other, and that as a result we will mature in our spiritual walk and, gradually, we will change.

"We will no longer live as spiritual lone rangers. Instead we will build a community where we can share our deepest thoughts and longings, secure in the knowledge that they will be treated with respect and held in complete confidence.

"God of all creation," he began, bowing his head and closing his eyes, "Everlasting, ever-loving God of our lives, guide us as we begin this journey together. We want above all to grow and mature as your servants, as we follow the example of your Son, who taught us to pray..."

They all joined in slowly reciting the Lord's Prayer. Cal was reminded of being at worship back in college, before he'd even thought about becoming a pastor. He was filled with peace, and he realized how much he missed being fed instead of always being the one doing the feeding.

Over boxed lunches, Tony asked everyone to reflect back on the time since their first meeting and share what it had been like to construct a timeline and to begin thinking about why God created them in the first place.

"Building a timeline of my life and reflecting on why God created me brought back so many memories that I haven't thought about in a long time," said Curt. "It showed me how God has used even what looked like setbacks at the time to help me grow deeper in my faith."

"Reading the scriptures you assigned and considering why God created me made me feel overwhelmed by the sense that God created me to be in relationship," said Juan. "God wants to be with me."

Rex spoke next. "It was a valuable exercise," he said. "It helped me see how God has shaped me through all the people and experiences of my life. Sometimes I've thought that my years in business were wasted—that I should have heard God's call to ministry earlier in life. Now I see more clearly how God used many of the people and experiences I had in those business years to shape me for the ministry I'm involved with today."

Cal shared that putting together his timeline had brought back a lot of wonderful memories. "It reminded me how much more alive I felt in my relationship with God during the years before I trained to become a pastor. It made me want to get that back. I felt a little of it when we prayed together just now, and that's encouraging."

Tony explained that the assignment they'd been working on over the past few weeks was designed to help them understand clearly their purpose for being on earth, their "reason for being."

"A statement of your reason for being will provide the first of three strands that together will make up your personal calling statement," he said.

Tony held up a three-stranded braid. Each strand was a different color. "I keep this on my desk to remind me of the three strands of my own personal calling statement: red for my reason for being, green for my values, and gold for my vision for the future.

"Remember the three big questions that the personal calling statement is designed to help us answer? Here they are again. Number one: Why did God create me in the first place? Number two: What beliefs, values, and passions has God been forming in me throughout my life? And number three: What might God be calling me to be and do with the remainder of my life?

"As I mentioned, we wrestled with answers to the first question—Why did God create me in the first place?—in order to begin to build our reason-for-being statement. Our timelines will help us find answers to the second question: 'What beliefs, values, and passions has God been forming in me throughout my life?'"

Tony asked the group to take forty-five minutes to go over their timelines as they answered questions on a worksheet that he handed out. The questions were designed to help them be aware of their values and how each of them prioritized those values.

"Try to identify your values and then list them in order, from most important to less important for you," he said.

Later, he had the men share what they had written down, and they discovered that even though they had listed many of the same values, each of them prioritized those values differently.

"Maybe that's by God's design," Rex offered. "Which means I probably shouldn't get so frustrated when someone on my consistory takes all eternity to understand the tiniest details about an issue before voting on it. Maybe attention to detail is a value that God put in that person as a high priority. It still frustrates the heck out of me though!"

They all laughed. Obviously Rex wasn't the only one who had experienced this frustration.

"It turns out that how we prioritize our values determines the second strand of the three-strand personal calling statement 'braid' that we're working on," said Tony. "Gaining clarity about our most important values helps us understand what God might have in store for us to do. Our values are closely woven with the first strand—our 'reason for being' statement.

"I've learned that you need quite a bit of time to process thoughts and insights about your values and how they are prioritized before you come to a firm understanding of your key values. Please think and pray about this over the coming month. Think about asking the people who know you best if they agree with your statement of values and how you have those values prioritized. Maybe others will add to your list or see that some values on your list are even stronger than you thought. Next time we'll talk about what we are learning."

For the rest of the afternoon, Tony talked about what he called "coaching." The concept was new to Cal. Tony shared that the kind of coaching he was referring to was about helping someone discover answers to the issues he or she was dealing with, along with opportunities for change and growth. He also said that God and the person's own knowledge and insights would provide the answers and direction, not the coach.

According to Tony, a good coach mostly just asked good questions and listened...and was comfortable with silence, and with answers and direction that might be different from what the coach might have thought was the way to go.

Cal thought that having a person like that in his life could be a real gift.

Tony went on to share that he believed each member of their network should have a coach, and that one would be provided for anyone who wanted one.

After taking questions about the coaching process, Tony mentioned that a coach he knew and regarded highly was willing to coach Rex and Juan if they decided they were interested.

"As I've mentioned, I'm also trained as a coach, and I'd like to offer to coach two of you: Cal and Curt."

Cal hoped his disappointment and shock weren't too obvious. Tony? Tony would be his coach? What was God thinking?

"Think about it. Pray about it," said Tony. "I'll be in touch with each of you in a week or so."

He switched gears and began to wrap up the meeting. They set a date for the next gathering. "Will someone volunteer to lead us in a time of worship at the next gathering?"

Cal felt a tug inside, but he was still distracted by the idea that Tony wanted to coach him. Before he spoke up, Rex offered.

"Thanks, Rex," said Tony. "Let's close with prayer."

Chapter Five
Getting Real

Over dinner that evening, Cal told Pam about the network meeting and explained the coaching concept that Tony had introduced.

"It sounds like a great way to help you sort out thoughts about what we've been talking about lately—basically, how to get the joy back."

Jordan and Jessica had helped clear the table and Cal and Pam were loading the dishwasher while the kids went upstairs to start their homework.

"I agree," said Cal. "Tony offered to be my coach." He tried to keep his tone casual as he poked spoons and forks in the silverware holder.

Pam seemed to see right through him. "What is it about Tony that bothers you so much?"

Cal sighed. "Well, for starters, he got the call to Third when we also had put our names in the mix."

Pam was quiet. This was old territory.

"And we've lost a few key families to Third."

Pam was silent for a few more moments before she asked, "Is there something that you know he's done that he shouldn't have?"

"Well, no. But it's still tough for me to like him...or trust him."

"Why don't you trust Tony?"

"Because it seems like good things happen to him at my expense."

"Hon, I doubt that Tony has ever done anything intentionally to hurt you. And now he's reaching out to you and asked you to join the network. Do you think this is really about Tony?"

"Ouch," said Cal. He moved to the dining room table and sat down. The last rays of a late winter sunset shone through the sliders.

Cal sat back and ran his hands through his hair. "I suppose this has more to do with who I am than with anything Tony has done. I guess I dislike him because God has blessed him with some things I've wanted."

"That makes sense," said Pam, "And, I have to admit that I like the idea of you and Tony working through things together. It could be a chance for some really deep healing."

"I've always said it's the tough times that force us to grow." He smiled. "I just hate it when my own words come back to haunt me!"

Pam stood behind him and massaged his shoulders. "Thanks," said Cal. "The truth hurts though." He turned to her and put on his best I-am-crushed face.

"Nice try. Let's go see how Jessica is doing with her science project."

* * * *

The next day, Cal sent Tony an email:

> Tony,
>
> I'm honored that you offered to coach me. Please let me know what I need to do so we can get started.
>
> Blessings,
>
> Cal

Tony responded:

> Great! I feel honored that you would trust me to serve you in this way. How about Arlens Coffee Shop on Wednesday at 10 a.m. for an initial meeting?
>
> Tony

* * * *

As he drove to Arlens, Cal was excited to begin meeting with a coach and a little anxious about sharing his insights with Tony. But mostly he was dreading doing what he knew he had to do: let Tony know how he'd really felt about him and that he was sorry for it.

The meeting turned out to be more of a pre-coaching session. Tony explained in more detail how the coaching would work. He also asked Cal what he hoped the outcome would be after six months and whether he preferred to talk over the phone or meet face to face.

Tony talked about his own expectations as well and jotted down notes about their conversation. He reviewed both of their expectations and asked Cal if he would be willing to treat them as a covenant, which Cal agreed to. They both signed the covenant, and Tony said he'd hold on to it in case they needed to refer to it later.

They set a date for their first real coaching session, and Tony asked Cal to think over the next few weeks about an issue or an opportunity that he wanted to explore in depth. Cal sensed their conversation drawing to a close.

"Do you have a few more minutes to hear about something I've had on my mind?" Cal asked.

"Go for it. I have fifteen minutes."

Cal gathered his thoughts as the server poured them another cup of coffee.

"If we're going to start this coaching relationship on the right foot, I have something you need to know about." He had Tony's full attention.

"I've held on to some negative feelings toward you over the past five years, and I've come to realize that was wrong of me."

"What was it that upset you?"

"I guess I've compared my ministry with yours and felt that because your church was growing you must be much better at it. A couple of families at First must have thought so too, because they left for Third, which only made me feel worse. It seems petty now, but bottom line, I was resentful of your success."

"I've never really thought about it until now," said Tony, "but I can see how it seemed like some of Third's growth was at your expense."

"Pam helped me see that my feelings toward you were really about my own insecurities, not about anything you ever did. We had a good talk after you asked me to consider having you as my coach. God has a sense of humor, don't you think?"

"Well, I sure do. This is going to come as a surprise, but I've been more than a little jealous of you over the years, Cal."

He smiled at Cal's puzzled expression. "It's true! You have a partner in life who is your partner in ministry too. That always struck me as a huge gift. And you and Pam seem to have a terrific relationship, both as pastors and as husband and wife. If you'll recall, I didn't do so well in the husband department the first time around."

"It never occurred to me...," Cal began. "But that's not something you need to apologize for. I want you to know that I feel bad about the way I thought about you. I've asked God to forgive me, and I'm asking you too."

"Forgiven and soon to be forgotten," said Tony. "Let's pray before we go.

"Father, thanks for this time we've spent together. Thanks also for helping us start off on the right foot in this new coaching relationship. We ask for your blessing on it. Help us grow in our obedience to you and our love for you and each other. In Jesus' holy name we pray. Amen."

They stood and gave each other an awkward but heartfelt hug.

"Just two weeks until the next network meeting," said Tony. "Right after that, we'll get started on the coaching sessions."

"I'm ready!" said Cal.

On the trip home, Cal thought about what Tony had said about envying his relationship with Pam. "It just shows another way in which I've been wearing a mask," thought Cal. His relationship with Pam had only been coming alive again over the past month. Tony could not have known that of course. He and Pam had never let anyone see how dry their marriage had really been over the past few years.

Cal had read that being a pastor put a lot of strain on the pastor's family—that a third of pastors believe that their vocation is an outright hazard to their family.* Cal wondered if families suffered even more when a husband and wife were both pastors.

He suddenly felt deeply shaken by the realization that they'd come close to living the flat life for years, maybe for the rest of his and Pam's lives. Or, God forbid, they wouldn't have survived as a couple. He whispered, "Thanks, Lord, for a second chance."

* * * *

Pam looked up from a book she was reading as he came through the front door. "Hon, what's wrong? Didn't it go well?"

"No. I mean yes. I mean, it did go well. Sorry, I'm not making sense."

He sat cross-legged on the floor in front of her. "Tony and I had a great talk. I let him know about what you and I talked about—about how I'd felt resentful toward him, and that you helped me see that the problem was with me not with Tony.

"I asked him to forgive me for the way I'd been thinking about him."

"And..."

"He was gracious and forgiving."

"But you looked so, I don't know, disturbed, when you walked in just now."

"I'd been thinking about us again, Pam. About how close we came to losing each other. I guess it shook me up pretty good. We've seen so many marriages go south. I'm grateful we get a second chance."

"Me too."

Just then Jordan bounded into the room and grabbed Cal's shoulders and shook him. "Dad, Dad, come outside right now!"

---

* *Pastors At Greater Risk*, by H.B. London Jr. and Neil Wiseman, Regal Books, 2003.

He smiled at Pam and turned to their youngest daughter. "Where's the fire?"

"Come on, Dad. No fire. The Bradys got a new puppy. His name is Fred. Dad, Mom, can I have a puppy? Please? You have to see him. He's really smart. He already knows his name."

Oh boy. The puppy thing again. "Okay, I'll go with you to see the puppy. But that doesn't mean we're getting a puppy."

He looked back at Pam as Jordan pulled him out of the room. "No puppy," she mouthed.

Later, over dinner, the can-I-get-a-puppy presentation continued. They all joined in a conversation they'd had a few times already, with the kids making their case, and Cal and Pam making theirs.

After a while, Cal just sat back and listened. The tumble of conversation was so ordinary, and somehow reassuring. Life was good.

* * * *

Cal began spending a lot of time thinking and praying about his reason-for-being statement and the beliefs and values God had been forming in him. He had times when he felt pretty clear about who God had created him to be, and sometimes even a sense of what God might be calling him to do.

Bright, warmer days hinted of the coming spring and pulled him outside for long walks. On a trek through nearby woods it struck him that his spiritual journey was like the partly cloudy weather that had set in that day. Sometimes, like the sun's warm rays, what seemed like God-given passion for making a difference in the world hit him straight on.

But then clouds of doubt would roll in—if he followed his passion, everything in his life and his family's life might have to change pretty drastically. Maybe he was already too far along in life to charge off in new directions. Maybe Pam was right: that was then, this is now. When these thoughts filled his mind, his enthusiasm turned gray and cool.

He walked for hours one afternoon, so deep in thought and prayer that he hardly paid attention to where his feet were taking him. As he crossed an open field toward a local shopping center, he ticked off his mental list of the things he valued most: Pam, the kids, time with God, loving others through actions not just feelings, being obedient to what God might ask him to do, hard work. Words embroidered on a pillow in a gift store window caught his eye: "The best things in life aren't things."

The words resonated. He wanted his life to reflect what he believed at his core: that life was about learning to love and serve people.

More and more he was taken with a deep desire to do something risky, something that might even seem dangerous. God would be with him and would protect him. At times he felt like his heart would explode with his desire to do something so big that it could only happen if God was behind it.

Exactly what the big thing might be was a mystery, but Cal knew that something inside him was shifting. It occurred to him that life hadn't felt at all flat lately—in fact it felt more like a world-class rollercoaster!

Chapter Six

"For I Know the Plans I Have for You"

The weather had dipped back to winter deep-freeze by the time the day for the third network meeting arrived. The forecast was for blowing snow, but Cal was glad Tony hadn't called to cancel.

As they sat down to eat lunch, Tony asked everyone to share what was going on in their lives.

Their updates stayed in safe territory. They talked about church programs, kids at college, and the pitfalls and promise of the newest information technology. It was nothing like the revelations that had come out at the end of their previous session together. Cal found himself hoping that their communication would turn deeper later in the meeting.

Their conversations carried past lunch time. Eventually Tony turned the meeting over to Rex to lead them in devotions. He read Jeremiah 29:11-14:

> For surely I know the plans I have for you, says the Lord, plans for your welfare and not for harm, to give you a future with hope.
>
> Then when you call upon me and come and pray to me, I will hear you. When you search for me, you will find me; if you seek me with all your heart, I will let you find me, says the Lord, and I will restore your fortunes and gather you from all the nations and all the places where I have driven you, says the Lord, and I will bring you back to the place from which I sent you into exile.

Rex asked Juan to read the passage again. Then Rex read verse eleven one more time.

> For surely I know the plans I have for you, says the Lord, plans for your welfare and not for harm, to give you a future with hope.

"I wonder what God's plan is for each of us?" he continued. "Let's spend time listening for God's plan. For the next ten minutes let's do a 'listening prayer.'

"Try not to ask God for anything. Try not to think of all of the things you need to do. Find a quiet spot and ask what God wants you to hear today, right now. Tie this to your breathing if that helps." Rex closed his eyes. "Gracious God…" (he breathed in) "help me hear…" (he breathed out). "Gracious God…help me hear…"

They all left the meeting room to find a place to pray alone. Cal discovered an empty classroom and sat on one of the chairs lining the walls. He tried to calm his thoughts so he could listen to what God might say to him.

His mind wandered to the next day's consistory meeting instead. It had been a long time since he just listened for God. "Gracious God," he said to himself as he took a slow, deep breath. He released his breath in a slow steady stream. "Help me hear."

He thought of the sermon he was working on. "Gracious God…help me hear." He thought about how much he loved Pam. "Gracious God… help me hear." Events from his college days flashed across his mind, events he hadn't thought about in a long time. "Gracious God…help me hear." Disconnected thoughts continued to rush through his mind…he couldn't hold on to any of them for long.

No pattern seemed to unfold. It was interesting to pull back the curtain on old memories, but he was disappointed that God hadn't seemed to reveal anything in all that mental noise.

When everyone had returned to the meeting room, Rex asked if anyone had heard something from God.

"It was hard to stop a lot of scattered thoughts from running through my mind," offered Juan. The others nodded in agreement. "I think it will take practice to calm my mind so I can listen better.

"Eventually I did get a sense of calm, a glimpse of peace. Then I had a strong sense that God has something different for me, that 'change is in the wind.' I know that sounds vague, but it's as clear as I can make it."

"It took me a while to get quiet too," said Rex. "At some point the words in Luke 18 where Jesus says, 'Let the little children come to me,' kept repeating in my thoughts."

"I wish I had something to offer, but honestly I didn't get a sense of God speaking anything to me," said Curt.

"I didn't get a clear sense of God revealing anything either," Cal said.

"And that's not unusual," said Tony. "We all have prayer times like that. I guess I simply had a sense of peace about us having started this network and that God plans to bless our times together in ways we can't even imagine."

They took a short break and then Tony drew the group's attention back to the Living by Design work they had been doing. "Pair up," he said, "and share with your partner the current version of the first two strands of your personal calling statement—strand one: the reason God has created you, and strand two: your prioritized values. Also, tell your partner whether or not you feel confident about the accuracy of these two strands in their current form."

Cal and Rex turned to each other and followed Tony's instructions. It turned out they both felt that their understanding of their purpose and values was becoming clearer but still seemed a little foggy.

Next Tony introduced an exercise designed to help them answer the question "What might God be asking me to do?" The answer, he said, would shed light on the "vision" strand of their personal calling statement, the third and final strand.

"I had no idea that Rex was going to use the passage from Jeremiah and provide a time of solitude for our devotions," said Tony. "It was a perfect prelude to our work together. It's just like God to provide exactly what we need just when we need it. As one of my favorite authors, Reggie McNeal, puts it, 'God loves to show off.'"

Tony asked them to remember what they had just reviewed with their partner and spend time wondering and writing about what God might be calling them to do in the next season of life. He gave the group forty-five minutes to do this. "Be sure to pray for God's leading," he added.

Cal looked over his timeline and values. He kept coming back to his college days. He had loved his time at Central University. His studies in pre-law had been engaging, but even more inspiring was the time he had spent serving with the Campus Light ministry. Through that ministry he had grown deeper in his commitment to Christ in his freshman year, and he had also met Pam. That year had been by far the most important year of growth and maturing in his life. He had learned to be a real disciple of Jesus, and he had fallen deeply in love with a woman who also loved God and, even more miraculously, loved him too.

By his senior year he had led a ministry of twelve underclassmen—young women and young men—who spent time getting to know people in the community who lived on the margins of society. Some were homeless, some were sick, some were just very lonely. The students would talk with them, pray for them, feed them—just generally show Christ's love to them.

He especially enjoyed taking donations for the ministry, buying dozens of breakfast sandwiches at the local fast food place, and bringing them into the core of the city on a Saturday morning. After a year or so, many homeless and hungry people would show up in the parking lot where he handed out the food.

At one point thirty or forty people came every Saturday, and many stayed for conversation, which sometimes opened up a door to talk about God's love for all people. For quite a few of them, Saturday morning was probably the only time all week that they learned about real love, thought Cal. He felt a tug of sadness wondering what had become of all of those men and women.

Cal had felt like he was making a big difference for Christ back then. He remembered being excited thinking that he might one day be a pastor. Then he would be able to make an even bigger difference for Christ.

But now that he was that pastor, it seemed like all of his time was consumed by what he called "administrivia." Even his preaching sometimes felt like a less-than-meaningful task instead of a chance to make a difference—a real difference—in people's lives.

The irony was not lost on him—after choosing to give his life in ministry he had actually moved away from the very thing that brought life to his ministry—serving people to show Christ's love.

He did serve people, but they were people who, although he loved them deeply, didn't seem to need him much. "They would probably be just fine without me," Cal thought. In college the people he had served had really needed him. His efforts had made a big difference in their physical, emotional, and spiritual lives.

He couldn't deny that many in his church today expected to be served rather than be available to serve. He remembered hearing a speaker at a conference talk about how people sometimes outsource their spirituality to their pastor and the church leaders.

So that was what was behind the flatness he had been feeling! No doubt about it. His passion came alive when he served alongside people who were on fire for Christ, people who wanted to reach out to serve "the least of these."

Cal tried to get back on track with the exercise. He tried to focus on what God was calling him to now, not what God had called him to in the past. But it was hard when the pull back to his college days was so strong.

When the reflection time was up, Tony asked each network member to share what he had experienced.

"I have a dilemma," said Juan. "I have a lot more clarity about the 'change in the wind' I sensed earlier, but I'm not so sure my wife is going to appreciate the way that wind is blowing!

"I feel God calling me to return to Honduras to use my skills as a builder. It's partly because I'm familiar with a ministry that desperately needs that kind of help right now. It's also because I want my four kids and my wife to be exposed to the work of God in a developing country.

"But my wife is CFO of the only hospital in the area. So, while I'm terrifically excited about the idea of returning to Honduras, I'm also terrifically worried about what my wife will think." He shuddered dramatically, and everyone laughed.

"It's something we'll certainly all pray about," Tony said. "But seriously, if God's calling you to do this, God will speak to her heart about it as well." The others murmured in agreement.

"Rex, what about you?"

"I couldn't get my mind off a program I just heard about called Kids Hope U.S.A. It's all about mentoring students—adult volunteers helping kids with homework and building healthy relationships with them. I'm convinced that God is leading me to launch this ministry at God's Community."

"I've heard good things about Kids Hope," said Tony.

"I went through the process of writing a personal calling statement when I trained as a pastors network facilitator," Tony continued. "Before I started the training I had sensed that God was calling me to start a network; that was confirmed in the training, and again today."

His voice grew husky. "For now, my passion is for my church and also for this group of brothers. I feel truly blessed that we have this place where we can show up and be loving and real with each other."

It was quiet for a few moments. Tony spoke again. "Cal, what about you?"

"I have to say that in many ways I feel like I'm in the right spot," said Cal. "I love our congregation and being a co-pastor with Pam. But something about life hasn't seemed right lately.

"At our first meeting I talked about feeling flat—like the spark had gone out of life—and that I felt guilty because I know that the way I feel is affecting my ministry and my family.

"Back then I told you I'd been feeling this way lately, but really it's been going on for a few years. When I spend time reflecting on my timeline, I feel a strong desire to go back to my college days, when life was anything but flat. I know our time today is intended to help me look forward, but my college experiences keep pulling me back there."

Juan spoke. "Cal, I wonder if your future might somehow keep you at your church but also somehow move you toward the things you used to experience in college."

Cal felt like a key piece of a puzzle had fallen into place. "I really think you're on to something, Juan!" he said. "I think that's a really important observation. Thanks!"

It was Curt's turn. "Curt, as you've reflected on your timeline and values, what do you sense God calling you to do?" asked Tony.

Curt looked briefly at each of them and then closed his eyes. He lowered his head into his hands. He sat in silence, and they all waited quietly. Cal prayed inwardly that God would give Curt courage and the rest of them wisdom.

Chapter Seven

Back to the Future

Tony broke the silence. "We want this to be a safe place for you, Curt."

Curt nodded but he didn't look up.

"Would you prefer to pass this time around?"

Curt nodded again.

"I don't want you to feel rushed," added Tony. "Take all the time you need."

When Cal asked Curt if it would be okay if they prayed for him, he nodded again. One at a time, each man laid a hand on Curt's shoulder and prayed with him.

"Father, help Curt open his heart and his mind to your guidance."

"Please, Lord, help us find the words and the courage to work through whatever we need to do together."

"Thank you, Lord, for a place to be honest as we honor you. Please complete the work you have begun in us. We want to honor you and glorify your name."

"Spirit, give us the wisdom that comes from above."

Tony was last to pray. "The words that come to my mind are 'Be still and know that I am God...I will be with you through all things...seek me...be still, my son.'"

"Thank you," said Curt. He looked a little less distraught. "I want to share everything that's going on inside, but I'm not there yet."

"It's really okay," said Tony. "When it's the right time, you'll know it. And if you need to talk with one of us before the next meeting, be sure to let us know.

"It's almost time to close. Before we do, take a few minutes to write down what you've learned about your purpose and vision today. This is the first step in what's likely to be a long process of discernment. Over the next month, pray about the vision, values, and reason-for-being statements that you're working on, and write down any thoughts or ideas you have that relate to them.

"Continue to work on putting your calling down in words, and think about talking it over with your coach in your next coaching session," he said.

Tony asked Cal if he would offer a closing prayer.

"Lord, we love you and we long to serve you," Cal began. "We often fail and allow our selfishness and brokenness to get in the way.

"Please help us to hear you over the coming month. Please help us tear down the walls that block your voice from being heard. Prepare us to follow you wherever you may lead.

"Thank you for this group, and for your call on Tony to lead it. Please bless each one of us over the coming month, so that we may meet again and pursue your call on our lives.

"Please do your work within all of us, that we would know your peace and align with your purpose and call on our life. We ask that you keep us safe until we come together again to offer each other support and love. Jesus, we love you and pray in your holy name. Amen!"

As Cal drove slowly home through the worsening snowstorm, he found himself repeating several times, "What a powerful meeting!"

It had felt great—and humbling—to be able to care for another pastor.

He could hardly wait to find time to think about what Juan had brought up. He also felt compelled to find time to talk with Pam, and to spend time in prayer, especially for whatever was going on with Curt.

He popped into his office for a half-hour to check on things and then headed home. He had to get a running start to get the car into the driveway, which was covered in drifts. When he walked through the door, Pam, Justin, and Jessica were cooking a stir-fry while Jordan sat in the family room watching a video.

"Hi, guys! If you want, I'll help Mom finish dinner." He gave Pam a hug and a kiss as the two older kids shot upstairs to their bedrooms. "How was your day?"

"Good. I got a lot done on next week's message. And I heard from Janie. She's going to take over keyboarding and formatting the weekly bulletin. Yea! She's set up with the right software and she's good with grammar and editing. Should work out well."

"Great news," said Cal. "And I've got network stuff I need to talk with you about. But let's finish dinner and eat first. I'm starving!"

Later, as they all dug into chicken, vegetables, and rice, the kids talked about their day at school. Jordan had gone on a class trip to the art museum and said someone had told her that a Dutch artist had cut off his ear. Was that true? Why would he do that? Jessica had learned that one of her best friends was moving at the end of the school year. They had promised to call and email each other forever. Justin wanted to talk about snowboarding lessons for next year.

Cal fired up the snow blower after dinner and spent the good part of an hour clearing the drive and walkways. It was hard to believe that spring was just over a week away. As he worked he thought about Curt and said a few prayers on his behalf.

Back in the house, he felt bone tired as he peeled off his heavy coat and untied his boots. It was quiet. He lay down on the sofa, pulled up an afghan, and fell asleep in minutes.

Someone was shaking him gently. "Hey."

Pam's face came into focus close to his. "Whoa. What time is it?"

"Just past ten. The kids are in bed. You looked like you really needed some rest, so I didn't wake you."

"Thanks. You're right. I was exhausted."

"But I'm curious about what you mentioned earlier about the network. Do you still want to talk?"

"Sure." He sat up and Pam took a seat at the other end of the couch and pulled her legs up. "We each found a quiet place in the church and took time to listen to what God might say to us. To help us get direction on the purpose statements we've been working on. At first it didn't seem very helpful. My mind wandered a lot."

"I always have a hard time with that—with quieting my thoughts," said Pam.

"Memories from our college days kept surfacing, but at the time they just seemed like another distraction. I wanted to see ahead to God's purpose for our lives, not back," Cal continued.

"Then, afterward, we all reflected on the highlights of our past to try to shed light on the plans God might have for our future. I felt frustrated because once again I could only think about college—about our time with Campus Light: really getting to know Jesus, worshiping with the other students, those times we spent with folks downtown…meeting the love of my life."

"That would be me."

"That would be you." He grinned.

"So you didn't really get any sense of what the future direction might be."

"Well, what's neat is, I did. All of that time I was frustrated by feeling caught in the past, I think God was trying to give me direction for our future."

"You're losing me."

"It took Juan to light the spark. Juan wondered if my future might somehow keep me at this church but at the same time move me toward the things we used to do in college. Boom! It hit me. I swear my heart started beating twice as fast. I still have no idea where this is going, but I'd bet top dollar that it leads to a vision for our future. What do you think?"

Pam nodded and smiled. "Those college days were some of the best times in my life too. I've had them on my mind a lot lately. Just the other day I was thinking, why can't life be more like it used to be for us? We were incredibly busy, but I didn't feel stressed like I do now. We had passion. We were making a difference. It was exhausting, but I never got headaches like I do now.

"How amazing would it be to do that kind of ministry again?" Pam stood, walked to the window, and turned to face him. "How cool would it be to have our kids be part of it? Now you've got my heart racing too!"

Pam grabbed a pillow off the chair next to her and tossed it at Cal. "Let's do it!" she said.

Cal caught the pillow one-handed and sat up. "Are you serious?"

"I am way serious. Serve the needy, feed the hungry, be present with the lonely. Let's do it and include our kids."

Cal played devil's advocate. "But we have a church to serve, we have a family to feed, and we need to keep a roof over our heads. We can't just go off and do what we used to do; there's no money in it."

Pam leaned forward. "Remember when we used to go into the city on Saturday mornings to serve breakfast?"

"That was my favorite part of the ministry," he said.

"Well, we could do that again, couldn't we?"

"Sure! That would be great. At least it's a start. At least it would feel like part of our ministry made a difference."

"That's what I mean by let's do it. Let's do it!"

They sat and prayed together, thanking God for their past and their present, and asking God to guide them into the plans God had for their future.

Later, Cal lay in bed unaware of the wind howling outside his window. His mind was working out the details: how much the Saturday morning ministry would cost, the logistics of getting the food, where they would set up, how to establish their presence, how they would start to meet people in the city.

He wondered if they needed to worry about their safety, and what the kids would say and think. He tried not to disturb Pam, who was sound asleep.

There were a lot of things to consider, but for the first time in a long time, Cal was excited about the future. He didn't sleep much, but it didn't matter. He felt ready to take on the world.

Chapter Eight

Let's Get Started!

During the next two weeks Pam and Cal gradually introduced the kids to the Saturday morning idea, and they seemed to think it would be fun.

"Could I bring Mark?" asked Justin. Mark was his best friend.

"We need to work on getting organized first," said Pam. "But if things go well, maybe in the future."

At last their Saturday to go downtown arrived. The kids grumbled when Cal and Pam called them downstairs at 6:30. Cal hustled to make enough coffee to fill a big insulated jug. He grabbed juice boxes for the kids and tossed them in the carton of supplies he and Pam had packed the night before. By 7:00 they were out the door.

Cal was grateful that the sun was rising in a clear sky. After the freak snowstorm, the weather had turned spring-like again, and Saturday's forecast had called for highs in the 60s.

The kids were still groggy when they pulled into McDonalds. They ordered a dozen breakfast sandwiches to take downtown.

At this time in the morning it was easy to find a spot to park alongside City Central Park, where they'd decided to set up. They piled out of the minivan. Justin grabbed the bags of food, Cal carried a folding table, and Pam lugged the jug of coffee. Jessica and Jordan followed with the carton that held the juice, a table cover, paper napkins and cups, cream and sugar, salt and pepper shakers, and coffee stir sticks. There was a jar of salsa in there too. Justin loved salsa with eggs.

They decided to set up the table on an open expanse of granite paving near the park's central fountain. They would be easy to see but wouldn't have to deal with the still-soggy grounds.

"I'm starving," said Jessica as she dug out a sandwich and grabbed a juice box. A man walking by just a few yards away glanced at her out of the corner of his eye.

"Hey mister, would you like a sandwich too?" called Jordan.

The middle-aged man in a stocking cap turned to look at them. He was wrapped in layers of sweaters covered with a well-worn jacket. He seemed to be sizing up the situation. What was this family doing here at this time on a Saturday morning? Why would the parents seem to be okay with the little girl talking to him, much less offering him something to eat?

Cal broke the silence. "We have extra and we're happy to share with you. If you feel like joining us, we'd like that too."

The man's expression was still guarded, but he walked toward them. "I'm Ralph."

Pam offered Ralph a breakfast sandwich, which he accepted.

"There's hot coffee," said Cal, holding out a cup he'd just poured. Ralph took that too and set it down on the table while he unwrapped his sandwich.

"I'm Cal. This is my wife, Pam, and these are our kids, Justin, Jessica, and Jordan."

"Pleased to meet you," said Ralph, taking a bite of the sandwich.

"Are you homeless?" asked Justin.

"I'm sorry..." Pam began, but Ralph interrupted.

"No, that's okay. Kids are great that way. Yes, I'm without a place to live right now, but I'm doing all right. It sure is nice of you to share breakfast with me." The sandwich disappeared in a few quick bites.

"Would you like another?" asked Pam, handing Ralph a napkin.

"Yes, ma'am, I would." He took a sip of coffee and seemed to relax a little.

"Do you know anyone else who could use breakfast? We brought plenty of extras."

"I can think of two friends, if you have enough."

"We do," said Pam. "Why don't you have them come eat while the food is still warm."

"Thank you, I will."

Ralph returned a few minutes later and introduced Deborah and Sam.

Deborah stared hard at Pam as she handed her a sandwich. "Is this some kind of church thing?"

Pam held her gaze. "Well if you mean did somebody from a church tell us we needed to do this, then the answer is no. But if you mean did Jesus ask us to do this, then the answer is yes."

"I suppose you all hear Jesus talking to you," Deborah said.

"Well, in the Bible he tells me that you're my sister, and that Ralph and Sam are my brothers," said Cal. "He also says to take care of each other and show kindness to all people."

Deborah was still wary. "Are you going to ask us to do something?"

Pam said, "No, we just believe God wants us to do this."

"So if we just get up and walk away without talking with you about God and how he is so wonderful, and how I need to follow your rules…you'll be okay with that?"

"You bet. But you're welcome to have some coffee too."

Some of the edge dropped from Deborah's voice, and she smiled. "Thank you, I believe I will."

The kids were done eating and had started a balancing contest on the benches surrounding the fountain as the five adults sipped coffee and made small talk.

It was mid morning by the time Ralph, Deborah, and Sam started to leave. "Thank you for your kindness," said Sam. "And don't let Deborah fool you; she's a sweetheart."

"You're welcome," said Pam. "Before you go, is there anything you would like us to pray about?"

"No thanks," said Ralph. "I really have to go." He turned and walked away.

"Pray that the weather stays nice," Deborah said. "That storm last week nearly froze us to death!"

"You can pray that my son stays off drugs," said Sam. "He's on probation and I can't stand to see him back in jail."

"Would you like us to pray right now with you, or later?" asked Cal.

"Later," Sam and Deborah replied together.

"We'll be right back here next Saturday, and I hope we see you again," said Pam. "If you know others who would like to come, we'll try to have plenty for everyone."

"We'll see what the day brings," said Deborah, and she and Sam started off in the same direction Ralph had taken. Just a block away they turned a corner and were gone.

Cal, Pam, and the kids threw their trash in a nearby barrel and packed everything up.

"What did you kids think about this morning?" Cal asked as they drove home.

"I like Ralph," said Jordan. "I think he was really hungry."

"It was pretty cool to bring food to people," said Justin. "But I feel bad that they don't have a home. Why don't they have a place to live and make breakfast, Dad? Did they do something bad?"

"I don't know about those three people, Justin," Cal replied. "I just know that lots of people who are homeless didn't do anything bad. Some people just can't find a job that pays them enough money to buy food and pay their bills. Other people get real sick and have to spend all their money on hospitals and medicine. When they don't have enough to pay for a house to live in too, they sometimes have nowhere to go but out on the streets."

Jessica was quiet, which was normal for her. Finally she asked, "Do they have kids?"

"Well, Sam has a son that he asked us to pray for," said Pam, "but I'm not sure about Deborah and Ralph. Maybe we'll see them again next Saturday, and you can ask them."

Cal pulled into the driveway, and Pam suggested they take a few minutes to pray together. She opened by thanking God for the morning and for introducing them to Ralph, Deborah, and Sam. Jordan asked God to keep the weather nice, especially for Deborah.

Except for a bird singing, it was silent for a few moments.

Cal asked that God would be with Sam's son and that God would give him what he needed to deal with his drug problem. He also asked God to bless all three of their new friends during the coming week. He praised God, the great lover of all people and thanked God again for all of the blessings poured out on their family.

As the kids jumped out of the car, Pam asked, "Should we do this again next Saturday?"

All three kids agreed that they should. "Does it have to be so early, Mom?" asked Justin.

"We'll see."

"Can Mark come next week?"

"We'll think about it," Pam and Cal said in unison. They laughed. It had been about as perfect a morning as they could have imagined. It felt like old times, only better. They were doing this as a family.

During church the next morning Cal realized he felt different inside. Everything about the service was pretty much the same as it had been every Sunday for the past five years. But, he thought, connecting with his passion the day before had rekindled his enthusiasm for ministry.

After the service and the fellowship that followed, Cal found himself looking forward to the new week and another trip downtown on Saturday to see what God had in store.

Chapter Nine

It's Alive!

On Monday, Cal and Pam took a day of Sabbath. After getting the kids off to school, they sat down at the dining room table to do a devotional together. They read several passages of Scripture and ended with Mark 8:35—"For those who want to save their life will lose it, and those who lose their life for my sake, and for the sake of the gospel, will save it."

"In other words, if you will let go of your life you will gain it," said Pam. "It's hard and more than a little scary to let go of my life. I need to keep reminding myself that the God who calls us to let go of our lives is the same God who loves us and promises to provide for us."

"Our lives and our kids' lives are definitely going to change if we pour ourselves into this new direction in ministry," said Cal. "In some ways I think we'll learn the same lessons we learned through college ministry all over again but in a different context."

"It's such a nice day. Let's go to the county park and hike around the lake," suggested Pam. "We both think better as we walk."

"Let's go," said Cal. It would be great to enjoy the outdoors together—something they both loved to do but that had been pushed aside too often lately.

They ate a quick lunch, laced up hiking boots, grabbed jackets, and headed out the door. It was only a few blocks to the trailhead for the path that hugged the shore of Little Pine Lake. They were mostly quiet as they walked, taking in the birdsong and enjoying the warmth of the spring sun. Cal felt a deep connection with God and with Pam.

At the end of their hour-long hike they sat down on a bench overlooking the lake. Cal pulled Pam close, and they both shut their eyes and tilted their heads back to soak in the sun. Pam began a prayer. "Thanks, Lord, for the incredible blessing of this day, for our healthy and loving family...help us be a blessing as we serve people who live on the margins in our community."

They were silent for a few moments. Then Cal added, "Lord God, continue the good work you have begun in us. Give us clarity to discern what you want us to do and courage to do whatever you ask us to do."

"Amen," said Pam.

Cal and Pam headed home so they'd be sure to be there when the kids got back from school. "I'm going to check email," said Cal as they walked into the house.

"I've got reading to catch up on," Pam said. She gave him a quick hug and headed for the family room. "And I'll make a grocery list for you for dinner."

Cal fired up the computer. The words "You have 18 new messages" flashed on the screen. One was from Tony, reminding him of their upcoming coaching session. Tony asked Cal to think and pray about what would be most important to discuss.

"That's a no-brainer," Cal thought. "What do we do with this new energy and vision for Saturday mornings?"

* * * *

Cal's second session with Tony was their first real coaching session.

Tony opened with a brief prayer asking God to give him the ability to listen well and serve Cal in a selfless way. He also asked God to help Cal hear what God might say to him on the topic they were about to explore.

"So, Cal, what is the most important topic we should explore in our time together?"

"Do you remember when Juan asked me how the kind of ministry I did in college might be part of my future as well? His question got me thinking in a new way about why I'd been so drawn to reminiscing about my college ministry days.

"I think it was God's way of leading me toward some kind of similar ministry today. I have a long way to go to figure out just what that looks like, and that's what I want to explore further in our coaching sessions."

"That gives us our focus, which is great," said Tony. "Tell me all you can about what you've learned so far."

Cal spent a few minutes catching Tony up with everything that had happened since he'd talked with Pam about his reaction to Juan's question. "We are open to God's leading and excited to see what takes shape," he concluded.

"This sounds exciting and I can see that it sparks new life in you," said Tony. "What else might God be telling you?"

Cal paused. He had been so excited about this first step that he hadn't really thought much beyond it.

The silence felt a little awkward, but Tony had learned in his training that in a coaching session the best work often gets done during times of silence. He remembered a phrase from *Fierce Conversations*, a book he'd read recently: "Let silence do the heavy lifting."

Tony remained silent, allowing Cal time to pull together several threads and begin to weave a coherent pattern.

Finally, Cal spoke. "I don't quite know what God wants to show me about what comes next. I do have a strong sense that it's supposed to impact our congregation somehow. I'm just not sure how at this point."

"Give me an example of what 'impacting the congregation' might look like."

Cal reflected for a few moments. "Somehow the joy that Pam and I are starting to feel needs to be shared—experienced by others in our congregation. Maybe we should offer to take a few people along with us."

"If you did, how would that work?"

Cal hesitated. "I don't know." After about thirty seconds he said, "Maybe we could invite a handful of people that we think would 'get it'—people who would understand why we're doing this and who might be interested in joining us. We could at least give that a try."

"What else might God be telling you?"

Again, silence. Then Cal responded confidently, "This is a good next step. God may have more for me, but I feel good, and I think God is giving me that feeling, that this next step is enough for now."

"Who are some of the people you might consider approaching?"

Cal began listing people that he thought might enjoy joining them on Saturday morning. He came up with a dozen people right away. Tony could sense Cal growing in clarity and confidence.

As their coaching time drew to an end, Tony asked, "What are you planning to do with what we have discussed?"

"I'm committed to talking with Pam about this idea, and if she agrees with me, then we will invite at least three people, and we'll see what God does with it from there."

"On a scale of one to ten, how committed are you to doing both of those things?"

"Ten!"

It was true. He could hardly wait to get back home to talk with Pam.

"Great!" Tony said. "I look forward to hearing all about it next month."

They set a date for their next coaching session and ended with a prayer of thanksgiving.

"Thanks," said Cal as they walked to their cars. "That was a big help."

"It was a good session," said Tony. "You've obviously been doing the work!"

Chapter Ten

Teamwork

Before he even started the car, Cal got a hold of Pam on his cell phone. He wanted to talk with her about what he'd covered in his coaching session. He also thought they could use a little time together without the kids.

"Hey, let's get a sitter and go out for dinner. I'll call John and Marie and see if Stacey can watch the kids."

"I love that idea. I'll stop at the video store on the way home and pick up a couple of movies for them."

They drove to Tandoori Kitchen, their favorite spot downtown. Over curry and naan bread, Cal caught Pam up on his session with Tony.

"Mostly Tony asks questions and then just listens," he said. "Sometimes it feels awkward because I have to take time to think about the answer to a question he's asked. Tony just lets the silence be. He wants the answer to come from me."

"That's commendable," said Pam with a grin. "I know how hard it is for you guys not to jump in with a solution when someone brings up something they're struggling with."

"Okay. Just eat your curry." He grabbed a forkful off her plate. "It's excellent."

"No, really. I can see how having someone let you find your own way toward an answer could be really valuable. So what did you learn?"

"That's what I wanted to talk with you about. I'm wondering if the next step for us to take is to find a way to let others in our congregation share what we're experiencing on Saturday morning. I had the sense that's what we need to do, but I wanted to check to see what you think."

"Absolutely. I've already been thinking about that. There are so many reasons to do it. On a practical level, there are going to be more people coming for the food and conversation, and we won't be able to keep up. Also, we need to give people the chance to grow by interacting with folks they've only seen from a distance."

"I told Tony that if you agreed, we would choose three people to begin with. Does that seem reasonable?"

"I think so. That way we can introduce things gradually and see how it grows. That's how it worked in college, remember? As people got excited about ministry they told others and it kind of took on a life of its own."

Before their rice pudding arrived they had agreed on three people they'd ask to join them. They chose Karla, a good friend of Pam's who lived nearby and was in Campus Light with them back in college. They would also invite a young couple, Al and Renee. Anytime First Church had sponsored a service day to stock the local food pantry or rake leaves for senior citizens, Al and Renee had signed up and shown real enthusiasm for the work.

On the way home, Pam drove past City Central Park. It was growing dark, but they could make out the shapes of a few people walking past the fountain where they'd handed out breakfast. Pam pulled to the curb and they watched as a patrol officer approached the people and gestured for them to move on. The officer was only doing what the city park rules and regulations demanded, but Cal couldn't help but wonder where those people would be spending the night.

"It will be good to get down here again on Saturday," he said.

"It sure will," said Pam. She turned back into traffic and they drove home.

* * * *

The following day Pam called Karla. She told her all about the new Saturday morning outreach. Would she be interested in joining them this Saturday at the park?

"I'd love to help out. It sounds like old times," said Karla. "But I have good news and bad news and more good news."

"Okay, Madame Mysterious, out with it!"

"I got that new job I told you about."

"That's very good news."

"The bad news is I have to work on Saturday mornings."

"Oh, that's disappointing. I really wanted you to be part of this. So what's the other good news?"

"I'll be able to help buy the breakfast food. And of course I'll be praying for you too."

"Thanks, Karla. I knew you'd want to help out. Now tell me about your new job..."

They talked for another twenty minutes, and then Pam called Renee.

"Cal and I would like to get together with you and Al to talk about an opportunity that we thought the two of you might be interested in."

"Just so it's not a direct sales opportunity," said Renee, and they both laughed. Recently Renee had shared a few hilarious stories about her brief and disastrous career selling cleaning products out of her basement.

Pam assured her that it was something she would enjoy hearing about. They agreed that the two couples would meet Wednesday morning at 7:00 over coffee at Arlens.

* * * *

Wednesday at Arlens, Pam and Cal shared the story of Cal's network and his coaching and how they had both felt led to start a Saturday morning ministry to engage with the people of the core city.

"I can see the excitement in your eyes, both of you, when you talk about this new ministry," said Al. "Renee, what do you think?"

"I think we should create a cool name for this so that when it becomes a much bigger deal, which I believe it will, it will be known throughout the city."

"You're the marketing person, Renee," said Cal. "I'll bet you already have something in mind."

"How about calling it '5,000 Plus'? Jesus fed five thousand men, plus women and children, with only five loaves of bread and two fish. We'll be feeding many people in many ways over the coming years with resources that God will provide. And like Jesus, we'll be right there with the people, showing them God's love for them."

"Wow. That's beautiful, Renee. I vote for 5,000 Plus," said Pam.

"We have commitments we have to keep for the next three Saturdays," said Al. "But after that you're stuck with us. We're in for good!"

Chapter Eleven

Trouble in Paradise

Cal and Pam were up earlier than usual on Saturday, eager to get going. Surprisingly the kids hardly groused at all as they quickly got ready to go.

At McDonald's they bought extra sandwiches, hoping that more people would show up to share them. They parked in the same area as they had the week before, gathered up the food and supplies, and set up alongside the fountain again. It was cloudy and a little cooler than the previous week. Puffs of steam rose from Pam and Cal's cups of coffee and the kids' cocoa.

They heard laughter and turned to see Ralph and Deborah strolling up the walkway with a woman they hadn't met yet.

"Hey, Cal, Pam. Hey, kids," Ralph said, reaching to shake the hand Cal extended. "This is our friend, Katherine. When I told her about your family and our breakfast last week she said she'd like to meet you too. You all said to invite some others, so here she is."

Pam and Cal and all the kids said hi to Katherine and welcomed Deborah too. Jordan, always the social one, started to ask both of the women questions. Did they have kids? Did they want breakfast? Did they like cream and sugar in their coffee?

Meanwhile, Sam strolled up from another direction with Lewis, a friend he had invited to join them.

"Welcome," said Cal. It occurred to him that in a way that was a strange thing to say when he and Pam were the ones being welcomed to the place where these people lived.

"Does anyone mind if I offer a quick prayer?" said Pam. No one objected and she prayed: "Lord God, thanks for this day and for life itself. Bless this food and all of us as we eat together. We pray in your name."

Several voices said, "Amen."

While they were eating, Pam made it a point to learn more about Katherine and Lewis. Cal spent time talking with Sam, Deborah, and Ralph.

"Sam, have you heard any more about your son?"

"As far as I know nothing has changed with him. But thanks for asking." It was obvious that it meant a lot to Sam that Cal remembered his request for prayers for his son.

Jordan told Deborah that she had prayed for good weather, just for her.

"Thank you, little one. That means a lot to me."

Plenty of food plus plenty of hunger added up to lots of eating, small talk, and getting to know each other.

Later, as they finished up, Pam asked if anyone had something they'd like to pray about. Lewis mumbled thanks, good-bye, he needed to get somewhere fast. Sam and Deborah said sure, and Katherine just nodded. Ralph was silent, but this time he didn't take off.

Cal asked if each of them would offer their prayer right now, silently if they wanted to. They all nodded or said yes.

Cal bowed his head and began: "Father, thanks for this time we've had together and for all the ways you bless us."

"Thank you for not raining on us," added Jordan.

"Thanks for our new friends," added Jessica.

"And for the food," said Justin.

"Thank you, God, for this family," Deborah prayed. "I hope they keep coming downtown."

Except for the sound of traffic in the distance it was quiet for a while, and then Pam closed. "Thanks, God, for all of your children, and for a chance to get to know brothers and sisters."

Several voices echoed her "Amen."

* * * *

The next week seemed to drag by for Cal and Pam. They were anxious for Saturday to roll around again. Finally it dawned bright and warm, just like the first Saturday morning they'd ventured downtown.

Things at the park went smoothly at first. Everyone who had come so far except Lewis showed up, along with three new people.

"The whole family comes down every Saturday," Ralph told the newcomers.

"And these sweet kids even share their McDonald's goodies with us," said Deborah. She smiled and patted Jordan on the head. "This one even asks God to order up good weather for us."

After an opening prayer, as they dug into food and conversation, Cal happened to look up. A tall, thin young man in black jeans and a hooded sweatshirt was striding down the walkway toward the group. He had his hood pulled down over part of his face and wore sunglasses, which Cal thought seemed strange at this hour of the morning.

As the man drew closer, Cal could see that his hands were twitching. He walked straight up to Cal, and the group fell silent. Cal glanced over at Pam. She looked calm, but slowly moved to gather the kids close to her.

"I need money, man."

"I don't have any money for you, but you're welcome to food and coffee."

"No. I need money for a bus ticket. I know you have money. Maybe I ought to just take it from you. Do you think you could stop me?"

The man shoved his right hand deep in the pocket of his sweatshirt.

In a flash, Sam stood next to Cal. Cal was surprised to hear his own voice, firm and calm, saying, "I'm sorry. We have no money for you."

Sam stared hard at the young man. The thought flashed through Cal's mind that Sam would make a formidable adversary. He was even taller than the guy in front of them and looked like he was in great shape.

Ralph also started making his way over to stand with Sam and

Cal. The guy in the sweatshirt backed away a few steps. "Forget you, man!" he shouted. He turned and walked quickly away.

Pam broke the tense silence. "Cal, Sam, Ralph—you handled that really well." Now that the crisis had passed, Cal felt shaky. The kids stood still and quiet.

"No one will bother you as long as I'm around," said Sam.

"We won't let anyone hurt you all," added Ralph. "Especially punks like him."

"Thanks again," said Pam. "Hey, let's finish off this coffee and juice." Cal appreciated her calmness as she encouraged everyone to fill their cups and begin talking again. She gave the kids a box of colored chalk. "Show us some artwork, guys."

The conversation turned to relationships. Ralph shared that he wanted to pray for his wife, a woman he still loved deeply even though he hadn't seen her in more than a year.

They all stood in a circle as Pam prayed: "Lord, we lift up Ralph's wife, Anita, and ask you to be with her and bless her. Help Ralph deal with the pain this brings him and bring healing and reconciliation to their relationship."

Ralph wiped tears away with his sleeve when they had finished praying. "Can I help you bring stuff to your car?" he asked.

Cal had started boxing up the supplies. "Sure. That would be great," he said.

Deborah and Sam pitched in too, and in no time they were ready to go. They all oohed and ahhed over the drawings the kids had chalked on the sidewalk and exchanged goodbye hugs and handshakes.

The kids hung out the windows and waved as Cal pulled into traffic and started home. He watched in the rearview mirror as Deborah, Sam, and Ralph turned back toward the park.

"Dad, were you scared when that guy in the hoodie walked up?" asked Justin.

"I thought we were in a movie or something. Was he going to shoot us?" asked Jordan.

Pam and Cal exchanged glances. "I don't think so, Jordan," said Cal. "I think he was just trying to scare me."

Jessica was quiet. Cal asked, "What about you, Jessica?"

"I think you and Mom aren't going to let us come to the park on Saturday anymore. That makes me sad and kind of mad at that guy for doing that."

"Well, I feel bad about it, too," said Pam. "But I'd feel a lot worse if we put you guys in any danger. If something bad ever did happen, I wouldn't want you kids to be there."

"But Mom—Dad and Ralph and Sam would protect us," Jordan protested. "If I don't get to see Deborah again, I will be pretty mad!" She crossed her arms, stuck out her lower lip, and slid down in her seat for emphasis.

"I understand, Jordan," offered Pam. "Dad and I just need time to think about it."

Chapter Twelve

The Power of Community

Pam and Cal had Stacey over to watch the kids that evening while they took in a movie. Over coffee afterward, they revisited the events of that morning.

"I think I let myself get so carried away with the excitement of doing that type of ministry again that I skimmed over the risks too easily," Cal said.

"Taking the kids does add another dimension," said Pam. "It's a really positive thing for them and the folks we meet in the park. But this morning just scared the life out of me!"

"Even with Sam and Ralph stepping up, there's a chance the kids could be hurt," Cal said. "Or that they'd see things that they're too young to get a grip on." Cal felt a knot in his gut when his thoughts painted a few possible scenarios for him.

"I think we need to pray and think about what to do," said Pam.

* * * *

The kids were in bed when they got home. Pam drove Stacey home, and when she got back she and Cal prayed together in the family room.

"God, we sense clearly that you are pleased when our family gives and serves in this new ministry," Cal began. "We also fear that something terrible could happen because we minister in a place where people don't always play by the rules."

"We're grateful, Lord, that things didn't get out of control this morning," Pam continued. "But now our eyes are fully opened to the risks involved with serving you in this way.

"We want to protect our kids, and most of all we want to follow you. Please show us what to do."

That night, they half expected Jessica or Jordan to crawl in bed with them. What kid wouldn't have nightmares after what had happened that day? But as far as Cal and Pam could tell the next morning, they had all passed the night peacefully.

Sunday morning was the usual whirlwind, with no time to talk about what had happened, or might have happened, the day before.

In the afternoon the weather was glorious, and the whole family hiked around Little Pine Lake. Early wildflowers poked through the carpet of old leaves, and they spotted a mama duck sitting protectively on her nest in an offshore clump of the last year's dried cattails and reeds.

That evening, and for the next four evenings, Pam and Cal spent time praying about the 5,000 Plus ministry. Should they continue things as they were? Was it irresponsible to put themselves and the kids in harm's way?

On one hand, the ministry was clearly something that God had called them to do. They talked about the devotional they had done together a couple of weeks back, when God had given them a sense that God would be with them every step of the way. On the other hand, they both sensed that they could be dancing with the potential for disaster.

By Thursday evening, both felt a strong sense of peace that the two of them should continue the ministry. They prayed for protection and asked God to empower them for the work ahead and give them wisdom as they moved forward with it.

They still were unsure where the kids fit in all this. They talked about how, even though they had strong faith in God and that God would work through them in this ministry, they also knew that they could never determine what God might do or allow. God was sovereign and God saw the bigger picture in a way they never could. They agreed that they should take prudent actions like updating their will and reaffirming who would take care of the kids in the event something catastrophic did happen.

Walking this fine line—having deep faith in God while also feeling the need to direct God's response—had always been a struggle for Cal and Pam; but in this case everything felt right. They were released from their fears and could move forward with the ministry without any more questions or concerns about whether they should take part in it.

One question still remained: should the kids continue to be part of it? They decided they needed at least another week to make a decision. They asked a church family that lived three houses away if it would be okay for the kids to come over Saturday morning for a few hours. They were relieved when the parents said that would be fine.

On Friday, Cal called Al to let him know what had happened the previous Saturday.

Al didn't seem too concerned about the incident with the young man. "I'll let Renee know and see if it's an issue for her," he said.

"Remember," Al added, "we can't make it tomorrow, but we will definitely come the following Saturday. And I'd like to bring a friend of mine along if that's okay with you."

"You bet. I trust your judgment on who would be a good person for this kind of service."

* * * *

Right away when Cal and Pam showed up, their Saturday morning friends said it was great to see them. "We thought you might never come back," said Ralph. He asked where the kids were. When Cal and Pam said that they were playing with friends, they couldn't help but notice the disappointment in the group.

They knew that the people who came for breakfast rarely got to experience the purity and innocence that healthy kids can show others. The few kids these people saw regularly were growing up on the streets, which meant they were forced to grow up way too fast.

Ralph added, "It means a lot that you treat us like people. We sure don't want anything bad to happen to you."

"We have a lot to learn from you," said Pam, "and we're grateful for your love and acceptance. Now, let me offer a quick prayer and we'll eat."

While they were eating, Cal and Pam asked about Sam's son and whether Ralph had heard from his wife over the past week. Both reported no change. They also asked how the others were doing and if anything interesting had happened over the past week.

Cal felt that God must be pleased to see his children coming together and caring for each other. He was filled with warmth and a sense of peace. In his heart he knew they were doing the right thing.

A new member of the group, which now numbered about a dozen, asked why Cal and Pam came to the park every week. Pam talked about how God loves everyone, even though we don't deserve it, and said that coming to the park seemed like a good way to respond to God's love. It was a way to pass that love on to others.

Cal thought that those gathered expected Pam's words to be the start of a sermon, and they seemed surprised when they didn't get one.

Then, out of the blue, Sam asked, "How do you know there's a God, and that God loves you?"

"I can feel it," Pam said, "and everything I see reaffirms it. All of the blessings I have ultimately came from somewhere. As I look at my life I have to admit that Someone or Something is behind the design of it.

"As I've come to accept that, I've also come to be grateful for that. Our family chooses to celebrate the Giver of these blessings each Sunday in our church services. It seems the more we accept and celebrate God's love, the more we are blessed by God—not so much in material ways, but in deep-down-peace kinds of ways.

"I suppose I can't prove God's existence to anyone," she continued, "but there are not many really important things in this world, things like love and compassion and justice, that can be proven. This doesn't stop me from believing in them. It's the same with God, at least for me."

Cal nodded his head in agreement.

"That's as close to a sermon as I want to get this morning," she said. "For the rest of the morning, I just want to listen. Sam, what do you believe?"

"I don't know what to believe," he said. "I like what you say, but I'm just not sure."

"I appreciate your honesty, Sam."

After a brief time of requests and prayers led by Cal, they packed up to leave. As Cal and Pam were walking away, Ralph yelled, "Tell the kids we said hi. And that we hope to see them next week!"

Chapter Thirteen

Out the Prison Door

As the day for the next pastors network meeting approached, Cal was excited about sharing with the group all that had happened over the past month.

The meeting began with Juan leading them in worship. He read John 6:16-21, the passage about Jesus calling Peter to get out of his boat and walk to him on the water. "It takes deep faith to follow Christ," Juan observed. "So often the apostles, and almost everyone else, lacked the faith to fully obey Christ—to 'walk on water.'"

Juan concluded with a prayer that God would grant each of them faith and courage to obey God fully. All of the pastors joined him in a loud amen.

Next came time to share what had been happening in their lives since the last session.

Curt was quick to begin. "I think I need to go first this time," he said. "I don't want to be in the same spot I found myself at the last meeting." His comment brought understanding smiles from the others.

Looking down, he paused and took a deep breath. Cal thought Curt's eyes looked like he had been crying recently.

Curt's silence seemed to stretch into eternity, but no one interrupted.

"I need to confess some things to all of you.

"My life is in a crisis, an emotional and spiritual crisis.

"I've been having an affair." His voice dropped to a whisper. "With a single woman from another town.

"I almost didn't come today. I thought about never coming again—so I wouldn't have to face all of you. If it weren't for the emails you sent, and a call from Tony, I would not be here.

"I decided to take the chance that you might still support me, and that I might be able to survive this."

Tony passed Curt a handful of tissues, and he wiped tears from his eyes. "I know very clearly what God wants me to do. Even though I'm not sure I can do it, I decided to start that journey right after our last meeting."

Curt looked up to see how the others were reacting. Their expressions of concern and sadness seemed to open a floodgate of emotion in him, and his sobs made it impossible for him to speak. Tony and Cal moved closer to him and each placed a hand on one of his shoulders.

A few minutes passed, each man praying silently, before Curt spoke again.

"The day after our last meeting, I broke off the affair. I intended to tell Theresa that night, but the time never seemed right—not that night, or the next day, or the next...I finally told her last night. I knew I couldn't tell all of you without telling her first.

"She's devastated, of course. She's in shock and confused.

"She's scared...I'm scared...I don't want to lose her. I don't know why I did this. I want to make things right, but I don't know if I can."

Curt took another deep breath.

"I also shared with her that I might be addicted to Internet porn. I met the woman I've been seeing through the Internet. We're both into porn.

"My life felt dry and empty for a long time. One day a couple of years ago I was online doing a Google search and a site I never intended to visit popped up. Those images—I was ashamed, but I couldn't stay away. Before I knew it I was on a path that led me where I am today."

Curt broke down completely, and it seemed like he was shrinking before Cal's very eyes. He'd never seen anyone this distraught.

"I am hoping and praying Theresa will somehow see a way to not leave me," Curt managed to say between sobs. "To not give up on us, even though I have done these terrible things. I'm praying that she will stay with me as I go through counseling. I'm hoping she'll agree to go to marriage counseling with me."

Tony spoke gently. "Has she given you any reason to hope that might happen?"

"We're going to talk again tonight. I don't know...I don't know.

"I'm also hoping that you all will let me stay, that I can still be part of this network. I think I need it more than ever."

Tony spoke again: "I intend to support you, Curt." The others nodded or said yes to show their agreement. "It's part of our covenant," he continued. "You will always be welcome here, and this group will be a safe place to take off your mask and walk out of your prison."

Hearing that, Curt grew calmer. "Thank you. I've set up an appointment with Dr. Styles. He helped me a few years ago when I had a bout of depression. I begin my counseling with him next week. If Theresa is willing to go, I'll ask Dr. Styles to recommend a marriage counselor. Or maybe one of you can recommend someone."

"I know a couple of counselors I can highly recommend," said Rex. "I'll give you those names before we leave today."

"I'm going to confess all of this to my executive team tomorrow night," said Curt. "I'm scared about that. Tomorrow morning I'll write a letter of resignation to offer to them. And I'll ask how they want me to communicate, or not communicate, with the congregation.

"I need your prayers and support. I can't walk this path without it."

One by one Cal and the others each gave Curt a hug. He was struggling not to break down again. Tony was last to hug him, and Curt seemed to hold on to him for dear life.

Rex offered a prayer lifting up Curt and asking God to bless him on the long journey ahead.

After Rex prayed, Curt said, "I know that this path will be tougher than anything I have ever had to endure. I can't put into words how much all of your support means to me."

Chapter Fourteen

The Truth Sets You Free

After a short break, they sat down to finish their meeting. During the break, no one had spoken a word. It wasn't an awkward silence though, Cal thought. The bond between all the men seemed stronger than ever.

"Curt, I know I speak for all of us when I say that I am thankful you chose to come to our meeting today," Tony began once everyone was seated. "It took great courage to share what you have told us. Thank you for trusting us, and for choosing us to walk with you as you work to get back on God's path.

"I want to share with all of you that I understand Curt's struggle with pornography on a deeply personal level. When I was going through my divorce, I was caught up in it too. It might have ruined my life if I hadn't had a mentor relationship with an older pastor. In our time together, God opened a way for me to confess what I'd been doing. I was brought to repentance, and my mentor and I set up accountability rules that I still stick to today."

On one level, Cal was shocked by Tony's admission. But on another, he understood how vulnerable pastors in particular were in this area. Recently he'd read a book about how prevalent depression, affairs, and other kinds of brokenness seemed to be with pastors these days.

"The statistics associated with pastors and pornography are alarming," Tony continued. "During our break, I pulled a list from a file in my office." He held up the list.

"Various surveys show that between 14 and 30 percent of pastors admit to having inappropriate sexual experiences. A 2007 Barna Research Group study found that 35 percent of men and 17 percent of women reported having used pornography in the past month. A 2000 *Christianity Today* survey found that 37 percent of pastors said pornography was a 'current struggle' of theirs.

"It's not a stretch to see why many pastors struggle with this. We work in isolation and usually without supervision. We often have no close friends. Most of us have easy access to the Internet."

Juan said, "I've read that pastors take antidepressant drugs at double the national average. It sounds like being a pastor is dangerous, and I am coming to believe more than ever that I should no longer risk being without support from a group like this one."

Rex continued. "I think Juan is right. We could all find ourselves in the same circumstances you are in right now, Curt. I want you to know that I'm not judging you, and I want to support you in any way that will be helpful. I will certainly be praying for you daily."

"Thanks, Rex," said Curt.

Tony said, "My hope is that having a network like we are creating together will make something like this much less likely to happen for any of us. I also hope the network and good counseling will help you get back on track with God, and with Theresa. We will be with you every step of the way."

He added, "Would you like us to go with you when you go before the executive team to offer your resignation?"

"Yes, that would mean the world to me."

"I'll be with you when you share what has happened with the congregation, if you think that would be a good idea," offered Rex. The others indicated that they would be happy to do the same.

"I don't feel like I deserve it, but I sure would appreciate it," said Curt.

* * * *

With the group's permission, Tony opened up time for each of them to share what had happened in their lives over the past month.

He started them off, telling about a sermon series that he had just completed called "The Missional Church."

"I'm excited about comments from some long-time members. I sense that they may be willing to consider what we as a congregation can do in the wider community, not just inside our own walls. Other than that, it was a pretty ordinary month."

Cal went next, and he shared both his passion and his fears about the new Saturday morning ministry. Tony said that he thought it would be good to spend time and energy discussing both. He encouraged Juan, Rex, and Curt to ask Cal questions about what he and Pam were doing and offer insights. Afterward they paused to pray for Cal and the new 5,000 Plus ministry.

Cal felt clearer than ever that he and Pam were doing the right thing. The increased clarity that came from his fellow pastors' questions and their clear support gave him greater courage and faith about this call. "If God is for me, who can be against me?" he thought.

Juan said he'd had a good month. He had shared with his wife what he had sensed about returning to Honduras to do ministry and was shocked by her response. She'd been having similar thoughts over the last few months!

She loved her job as CFO for Jefferson Community Hospital, so she had been trying to ignore those thoughts. But when Juan told her he'd been thinking along the same lines, she began to wonder if the call to Honduras might be a call from God. Together they'd decided to explore that possibility further with, as Juan put it, "obedient hearts and a sense of adventure."

Juan had spoken with his denomination about missionary work going on in Honduras. He had learned about a great opportunity to go there as part of a mission trip in the fall. "Our family is talking about taking part!" he said.

"You're almost as excited about Honduras as I am about 5,000 Plus," Cal said.

Rex had endured a tough month with the deaths and funerals of two long-time members of God's Community Church. "Even after wonderful celebrations of each of their lives at the funeral services,

I still feel a huge loss," he admitted. They paused to offer a prayer for Rex.

"Thanks for your support," he said.

They took another quick break and returned to share their progress in writing their personal calling statements.

Cal went first again. "My reason for being is to be the hands and feet of Christ in this world," he read. "I want to build his ministry with and around my family, and a big part of my ministry is to serve my brothers and sisters who find themselves on the margins of society."

He added, "The only piece I'm still wondering about right now is whether Pam and I should be involved with college students in some way. But that doesn't seem to be pressing right now."

Juan shared that he was clear about serving Hispanic people and that it would be important to include his family in this service. He felt a pull to serve people in Honduras and was looking forward to the possibility of the trip in the fall. "It will help me and my wife better understand what this call might really be," he said.

Rex said he felt a clear calling to continue to lead God's Community. He sensed God calling him to lead his congregation to look into ways they could reach out to young kids who were at risk. He suspected that Kids Hope U.S.A. would be a good fit for this. He already had a meeting set up with Kids Hope representatives to learn more about how it all worked and how to get a program started.

"Nothing has changed with my personal calling statement since I shared it with you last month," Tony said. "But I am more convinced than ever that we need to continue what we have started with this network."

Curt spoke last. "I need to get through what's coming and begin rebuilding my life before I can tackle a personal calling statement."

"I understand," said Tony.

"I have a brief announcement before we close," Tony continued. "I'd like to offer a Living by Design retreat for up to five people from each of your congregations. 'Personal renewal precedes corporate renewal.' That's the foundational truth of the Living by Design process we've been engaged in through this network. In other words, we've learned that if we are going to see our congregations revitalized, we need first of all to experience revitalization in our own lives, and then we need to lead people in our congregations through a revitalization process as well.

"During the weekend retreat, which you would attend along with the people from your congregation, we'll introduce people to the process of writing a personal calling statement. The retreat will be a kind of condensed version of what we've done together in our network.

"I can virtually guarantee that if people will commit to follow through on what they learn at the retreat, your congregations will begin to come alive in ways you won't believe.

"I have brochures for you to take to introduce the Living by Design retreat to your church leaders. Please have them call me if they need any additional information."

Tony handed each of them a handful of brochures and answered questions about possible dates for the retreat and how to decide who to invite. Everyone but Curt promised to present Tony's offer to their consistory and report back to him at the next network meeting.

Tony closed with prayer. "Lord, walk with us as we continue to explore who we are in you and where you are calling each one of us. Help us support one another. Especially help us give Curt what he needs from us during this difficult time. We love you Lord, and we thank you for this time we've had together."

Cal offered to lead devotions the next time they met.

Tony turned to Curt. "Before we leave, what time will you be meeting with your consistory tomorrow night?"

"At seven. My resignation will be the first thing on the agenda."

Curt thanked them again for their willingness to be there with him. They all walked together to a side door that opened onto the parking lot.

The warm, bright sun felt like a benediction to Cal. He turned to Curt. "Courage," he said.

Chapter Fifteen

The Journey Ahead

The next evening Cal, Tony, Juan, and Rex met in Church of the Savior's parking lot at 6:30 and waited for Curt. He pulled in 10 minutes later, and they all went to his office to pray. Meanwhile the consistory gathered in a downstairs meeting room, preparing for what they thought would be a typical meeting.

Curt and the other pastors walked to the meeting room, and Curt quickly introduced everyone. None of the consistory members asked why all of the pastors were there, but it was obvious they sensed this wasn't going to be business as usual. They sat looking expectantly at Curt. Cal thought Curt seemed pretty calm considering the circumstances.

Curt gave Tony a sad smile and looked down for a few moments before turning to the chair of the consistory. "I have something that I need to confess to all of you. I also need to offer my resignation."

The consistory members looked shell shocked. Curt continued. "Over the past half-year I've had an inappropriate relationship with a woman, someone I don't believe any of you know, and I've fallen into an addiction to pornography. One month ago I broke off the relationship. I have also committed to stop visiting inappropriate websites and to seek professional help.

Cal thought Curt seemed amazingly calm.

"Two nights ago I told Theresa, and I don't know what will happen with our marriage. I am prayerful and hopeful that she will give me a chance to rebuild what I've destroyed. I am committed to trying, but I wouldn't blame her if she chose not to.

"Yesterday I shared this with my fellow pastors from the network group that Tony started a few months ago, and they have embraced me." Now his voice became shaky, but he managed to keep his composure.

"They offered to be with me tonight as I confess to you and offer a letter of resignation."

One of the consistory members began to speak. Curt respectfully held up his hand. "Please, let me finish.

"I am terribly sorry for this on so many levels, not the least of which is the position that this puts all of you in. I hope that at some point you will be able to forgive me. With God's help and the support of these brothers here tonight, I am going to pursue a righteous path again, and I am ready to accept any consequences that need to fall on me.

"I have just one request—that we manage this information with the utmost sensitivity for Theresa's sake. I don't quite know what that looks like. I'm willing to openly admit my sins to anyone that you decide I need to admit them to, but I would appreciate it if the information came out all at once and in the most honest and accurate way possible.

"Thank you for letting me finish."

Tony added, "Before you engage this difficult time, please know that all four of us," he indicated himself, Cal, Juan, and Rex, "are committed to supporting Curt regardless of his consequences, and he has indicated to us that he's committed to pursuing the righteous path he mentioned.

"I also want to share with you some of the troubling statistics that show that pornography and other issues are a big problem for pastors."

Tony placed a stack of papers on the table. "I hope you'll read these. Please be careful about casting stones at our brother without first reading these articles. Thank you for allowing me to speak."

Curt asked, "Do you have any questions for me?"

One of the members of the executive committee, Tom Middleton, spoke. "This is a huge shock, Curt. I'm sure you realize that. We definitely need time to talk and reflect."

"Once again, I am so sorry," said Curt. "I'll leave you to decide what you would like to do. Tom, please call me tomorrow to let me know what you all have decided."

With that, Curt and the other pastors left.

It was nearly dark as they walked back out to the parking lot.

"Thanks guys. It helped to have you there."

"You're welcome to come over to the house for a while," offered Tony.

"I'll head home in case Theresa's willing to talk more. Plus, I'm exhausted."

"Goodnight, Curt."

They all called goodbyes and headed to their cars.

As he sank into the driver's seat, Cal felt tremendous weariness wash over him. The last couple of days had been draining even for him. He couldn't imagine how empty Curt must feel.

Chapter Sixteen
A Rare Gift

Pam and Cal had thought and prayed long and hard about whether or not to keep taking the kids downtown on Saturday mornings. In the end, they decided they would, mostly because they had peace that it was what God wanted.

Renee and Al were already waiting in their car when Cal, Pam, and the kids pulled up at the park. Amid hellos and hugs, Al introduced his friend, Roy, to Cal.

"Roy is a former police officer," said Al.

"Worker's comp issues put me on a desk job," said Roy. "I knew that wasn't going to work, so I'm security for the mall right now. I've been interested in urban ministry for years. Thanks for letting me join you today."

"Thanks for coming," Cal said. Roy's background in law enforcement seemed like another affirmation of their decision to bring the kids.

They were working together to set up breakfast when they heard Ralph holler, "Hey, strangers! How are you?"

Jordan ran down the sidewalk to Ralph, grabbed his hand, and walked with him back to the group.

Cal thought Ralph looked like he was on cloud nine. Jordan and the other kids definitely added a special warmth to their times in the park.

"Ralph, how are you?" said Pam, handing him coffee with lots of milk and sugar, just the way he liked it.

"Good, good. Pretty much like every week, except I wrote my wife a little note and left it in her mailbox. I prayed for her every day, too. And I prayed for you guys. I have to admit, I prayed the kids would come again." He smiled down at Jordan, who was taking it all in.

"Ralph, will you do art with me? Mom, can I have the box of chalk?"

"Sure, hon. But I'm not sure Ralph wants to do chalk drawings right now."

"Well, I'd love to," said Ralph, winking at Pam. "I was pretty good at art back in high school."

Pam handed over the chalk. "Have fun, you two."

"I'm excited to see what God will do here over the coming year," she said to Cal and the others as Ralph and Jordan began decorating the sidewalks a short distance away. She led them all in a brief prayer, and when they opened their eyes, they saw about a dozen people approaching.

"Howdy," said Deborah as they drew closer. "Meet some new friends."

"I'm Pam." Pam stepped forward. "This is my husband, Cal, and these are our friends Renee, Al, and Roy."

Deborah shook hands with Renee, Al, and Roy. "Pleased to meet you," she said and introduced the people with her.

As everyone helped themselves to food and coffee, Cal suggested that each person share one thing from his or her life that was really important to them.

"I'll go first," he said. "My wife, Pam, and my three kids are really important to me."

"It's really important to me that if I say I will do something, I do it," said Sam.

"That's important to me too, Sam," said Deborah. "Especially since you said you'd change your will so I'd inherit everything you own."

"Uh-huh. Now when did I say something that stupid?" said Sam.

"Just after you inherited all that oil money, baby."

Everyone laughed and started talking. The icebreaker hadn't gone as Cal had meant it too, but that was okay. The point had been to make people feel comfortable about talking, so in that sense it had worked.

Renee walked over to where Ralph and Jordan were still busy decorating the sidewalk with bright sticks of chalk. What she saw surprised her.

"Ralph, your drawings are amazing!" She caught Jordan's disappointed look and quickly added, "Yours too, Jordan. Wow! That puppy dog is really cute."

Jordan beamed and ran to get Pam to come take a look.

"Seriously, Ralph, you're very talented," Renee continued. The sidewalk fairly vibrated with the energetic geometry of abstract shapes and vivid hues that filled the sidewalk.

Ralph seemed a little embarrassed. "I always liked to draw."

"I work in marketing, and I sometimes choose artwork for our projects," Renee said. "Your work has a great edge to it.

"I have an idea. Al and I plan to keep coming here on Saturday mornings. We've been calling this breakfast time 5,000 Plus. Do you know the story about Jesus feeding five thousand men and many more women and children with just a few loaves of bread and a couple of fish?"

Ralph nodded. "Yes, ma'am. I remember that story from when I was a boy in Sunday school."

Jordan had pulled Pam over to see their drawings. She praised Jordan's flower garden complete with fuzzy black and yellow bees. Jordan crouched down and started filling in more color. Then Pam turned and took in Ralph's work. She was just as impressed as Renee.

"That's incredible, Ralph."

"I have an idea," Renee said again. "Why not use Ralph's art for a 5,000 Plus logo? I have a camera in my car. Ralph, if it's okay with you, I'll take photos of your work—and Jordan's too," she added as the little girl looked up. "Then I'll design a logo with your art in the background. Would that be okay, Ralph? I mean it's totally up to you."

"Are you kidding? It would be great! I've never had anyone want to use my art before."

Renee was back in a flash with her camera and took lots of shots from many angles. Everyone walked over to see what she was up to.

"You've been holding out on us, Ralph," said Deborah. "I never knew you were an artist."

Ralph made a few self-effacing remarks, but his friends were having none of it. Cal thought they all felt a sense of pride that Ralph may have looked like any other street person on the outside, but inside he had something rare and special.

When the coffee was mostly gone and it was almost time to leave, Cal asked for everyone's attention. "Let's finish our time together this morning by talking to God a bit. Anyone is welcome to join in with a prayer, or to just pray silently. If you need to leave and would rather just tell us about a few things you want prayed for, that's okay too."

Several people stayed and a couple of them prayed out loud. Their voices mixed with the sounds of traffic, and sometimes it was hard to hear what someone was saying, but the tone of their words and their bowed heads communicated powerfully.

As people said goodbye and wished each other a good week, Renee and Al smiled at each other. "I'm so glad we get to be part of this," said Renee.

"God is up to some really cool things on Saturday mornings in downtown Jefferson," said Al. "What about you, Roy? Do you want to come back?"

"You bet," Roy responded. "Helping folks was my reason for being in law enforcement in the first place. This takes me back to the days when I walked the beat not far from here. Getting to know people, putting a face on all the statistics we read about. Those were some of my best times on the force."

Sam had stayed to help them pack up. Cal noticed him staring at someone across the park who was watching them.

"That's my son, C.J.

"C.J., come over here. I want to introduce you to some folks."

C.J. walked slowly over to them. Sam quickly introduced everyone as Pam handed C.J. a bag with the last two breakfast sandwiches. He mumbled, "Thanks."

"You look good, son," said Sam. "I'm glad you came."

C.J. looked in the bag and gave his dad a quick smile before he turned and walked quickly away.

"I didn't think he'd come," said Sam. "Maybe God heard our prayers after all. I can see by his eyes he isn't doing drugs today."

Chapter Seventeen

Momentum Builds

On Sunday, Cal and Pam decided to announce to the congregation what was going on with the 5,000 Plus ministry. "Let's just let everyone know about it and see if anyone wants to know more, maybe even get involved," Pam had suggested.

During the part of the worship service set aside for announcements, she began, "As many of you know, Cal and I used to serve with a core city ministry when we were in college. In fact, that's where we fell in love with ministry and with each other.

"A couple of months ago, we sensed God directing us to undertake a casual ministry of food and community building at City Central Park. We started getting up early on Saturday, stocking up at McDonald's, and setting up a breakfast table for homeless folks who hang out in and around the park.

"It's been so rewarding. We're making new friends—about a dozen people come now—and once in a while God opens a way to minister with someone one on one. Last week Renee and Al came along, and they enjoyed it so much that they plan to start coming every Saturday.

"We didn't want to keep something this exciting to ourselves, but we did want to get a sense of the shape this ministry would take before we invited more people from First Church to participate. Cal and I agree that now it's time to open up this opportunity for ministry to everyone here at First. If you want to come along this week, or if you just want to learn more about it, please see me or Cal after worship."

No one asked her or Cal about the downtown ministry after the service. A few months ago that would have discouraged them. But Cal and Pam had no doubt that God was blessing 5,000 Plus. With the congregation or without it, they would continue the outreach ministry.

After church they took the kids to Little Pine Lake for a picnic. They spent a good part of the afternoon walking the trails, playing Frisbee, and kicking a soccer ball around.

"Look at this," Cal said to Pam on their walk home. He pulled his jacket aside and pointed to his belt. "I've had to take up two notches, with all the time we've spent walking and everything."

"I'll have to get you new khakis for Father's Day," said Pam. He made an exaggerated frown, and she added, "Really, it's terrific to see you getting back in shape. You look great.

"Life is good!" she said, grabbing his hand.

Cal nodded in agreement. "The new ministry is a big part of that," he said. "I feel like we've got our passion for people back, don't you?"

"I do. Do you think we would have gotten here if you hadn't gone through coaching?"

"I suppose it could have happened some other way. But when I could see clearly why God put me here—actually I should say when we could see clearly why God put us here—that was the key. The key to getting out of Flat World! It's pretty cool to think it all started with that email from Tony."

"And it's been really cool getting to know Ralph and Sam and Deborah," said Pam. "I believe God is ready to make a difference in their lives. And we get to be part of that."

Cal squeezed her hand. "It's just like old times. Except everything old is new again."

"Revelation 21:5. God makes all things new again," she said.

"Now you're going all eschatological on me."

"That's what you get for marrying a preacher. Now see if you can beat the preacher home." Pam took off running and Cal sped after her. The kids joined in too.

They ran all the way home and fell over breathless and laughing in the front yard. "The neighbors must think we're loons," said Pam between gasps.

"They don't think it, they know it," Cal said. "I think they'll get over it."

Once they'd recovered and gone inside, Cal and Pam settled down to read while the kids did homework. Later Cal decided to check his email and found a reminder from Tony. They had a coaching session on Thursday. Tony asked Cal to think and pray about what would be most important to explore in their time together.

This time is wasn't so easy to decide. Things seem to be going so well. What would be most important to explore?

* * * *

Cal thought and prayed over the next two days about what to tackle at the coaching session. He decided he should explore how the 5,000 Plus ministry might affect life at First Church, or how God want might want it to.

On Thursday, Cal met Tony in the same booth at Arlens where they had sat a month earlier. After the usual pleasantries and a brief prayer, Tony asked Cal what he wanted to explore.

"I'd like to gain greater clarity about how God might want us to use the 5,000 Plus ministry to impact our congregation and how that might be accomplished."

"Great. What thoughts come to mind as you consider how God might want you and Pam to use your new ministry to impact people at First Church?"

"Well, frankly, the obstacles to doing that come to mind first. We opened up the opportunity for folks to join us in the new ministry, and no one came forward. Pam and I have talked about this quite a bit. We think people want church to go on as usual. Most folks don't want to be pulled out of their comfort zone.

"We've also talked about how exciting it would be to integrate the new ministry with life at First Church. It would present great opportunities for the spiritual growth of our members as they minister to society's downtrodden and outcast people—the very people Jesus always reached out to.

"And the needs of the people downtown are great. They need to see God's people serving them in practical ways. Pam and I have seen this so many times in the past. People respond to the gospel when it comes to them in the form of people's hands and feet."

Tony continued to ask questions that called Cal to dig deeper for insight and answers. After forty minutes of exploration Tony said, "Okay, Cal. Now what are some of the options for moving forward?"

"We could ask for financial support for the ministry. We could ask for food and clothing donations. We could have a series of messages on what it means to follow Christ."

"Those are all good ideas. But I want you to go deeper. What option might God want you to see that you haven't identified yet? In fact, take a minute to ask God."

Cal closed his eyes and lowered his head. Silently he asked, "God, what else do you want me to consider as Pam and I move forward in ministry with people at First and the people downtown?"

Cal sensed God asking him to be patient. He also sensed that he and Pam should continue to serve on Saturday mornings and continue to invite anyone from the congregation who might like to join them.

In the quiet of his mind, he also thought God was saying, "Let it grow organically; then, over time, as others start to hear more about it, you will be in a great position to ask people in the congregation if they want to do something bigger with it. Let them pull it out of you rather than feeling like you need to push it on them. If they never pull, I will still have given you a wonderful ministry that is feeding you and my other children. You will still be making a very worthy difference for me."

Cal shared these insights with Tony and added, "This organic growth might lead to a time when we can ask everyone in the congregation to consider what else they might do to serve their brothers and sisters in the community. And what God might be prompting them to do for God's purposes and to bring them new life."

Tony asked, "Is there something specific you should do in the coming month regarding this?"

"I'd like to talk with Pam about who else would be good to invite to come along. Other than that I can't think of anything other than to just enjoy what God is doing through us right now."

"That sounds good, Cal. Would you close our time together with prayer?"

Cal thanked God for Tony, for the insights, and for all that had happened and would happen through 5,000 Plus.

That evening Cal and Pam discussed what he had learned in his coaching session. She agreed that allowing people to be drawn to the ministry was the best way to go.

"Organic is a good word to describe how it needs to grow," she said. "It has connotations of life, health, fruitfulness. By the way, has Renee shown you the logo she's designed using Ralph's artwork?"

He shook his head.

"I have it filed away in an email folder. Come see."

She sat at the computer and Cal leaned over her shoulder. "When you used the word 'organic,' I thought, 'How neat!' Because that's exactly what the logo communicates."

She clicked the mouse a few times and the logo popped up on screen. In vibrant green, red, and yellow stood a tree that, by its abstract shape, also suggested a cross. Fruit hung from the branches and its roots reached deep into rich, black earth. "5,000 Plus" was printed beneath the tree.

"Wow. Nice work. Renee and Ralph make quite a team."

"She plans to have a small banner made to tie to the serving table. What do you think?"

"Great idea. As the ministry grows, we'll find lots of ways to use this logo. The only thing I would suggest is showing it to Ralph first. He's the artist after all."

"Agreed. I'll call Renee and ask her to do that."

"Can I ask you something?"

"Sure."

"When you think about the future, are there things besides 5,000

Plus that you want to do?"

"It seems like some of Tony's coaching skills are rubbing off on you, Cal."

"That could be. But I'm serious. I know you're sold out to the new ministry, but what else do you dream about?"

"Well, it's funny you should ask, because I've been meaning to tell you that I'd like to learn how to start a pastors network, maybe one just for other female pastors."

"You would make a terrific coach. Look what you've already done for me!"

Pam looked him in the eyes to see if he was kidding around.

"I really mean it! You're a great listener, and you let me find my own answers. Well, most of the time anyway."

"Thanks, hon."

"Let's ask Tony how to find out about starting a network. I'm with you one hundred percent. And remember Marie, the pastor at New Life Ministries? She was invited to join our network, but the timing didn't work for her. As I recall, she was going to look into starting a network for female pastors. You should talk with her."

"Not quite so fast! I'd like to take a little more time to think and pray about it."

"No problem. It's a big commitment. You don't have to rush it. But how about just getting some basic information? It will help you decide."

"Sounds good. Now let's throw a couple of pizzas in the oven. I'm starving!"

"Me too!" the kids shouted in unison from the family room.

Chapter Eighteen

The Future Is Unfolding

On Monday morning, Cal had an email from Tony. It seemed like ages ago that he'd sat down at this exact hour and been wary of an email from Tony.

This email was a reminder that it was time for the network's fifth meeting. They had been meeting for five months. Incredible.

Cal remembered that they had committed themselves to meet for six months and then decide whether to keep going. He hoped Tony and the others would be willing to continue. So much good had come out of their times together. On the other hand, Cal felt like the changes he had seen so far—in his ministry, with Pam, and in relationships with other pastors in his community—were only the beginning.

The email from Tony also reminded him to bring the names of people from First Church who might be interested in a Living by Design retreat. Cal put this on his task list for the day. He and Pam had decided to find out if any members of consistory were interested in coming to the retreat and then, depending on how many elders or deacons expressed interest, to approach Renee and Al, and also Roy, who had started attending First about a month earlier.

Cal wrote an email invitation to the consistory members, and three of them responded with a "yes" later that day. Roy said yes on the spot when Cal called him. Cal was excited to think of what the upcoming retreat might mean for these leaders.

* * * *

Tony's email had also included a reminder that Cal had offered to lead devotions for the upcoming network session. Cal spent Tuesday morning at his church office trying to discern what God might like him to do with this opportunity. He spent time praying and listening for what God might tell him and sensed that God was leading him to focus on God's faithfulness.

Cal walked across the hall into Pam's office and sat down across from her.

"I offered to open with devotions at the next network meeting," he began. "My thoughts keep coming back to God's faithfulness. When you think about God's faithfulness, what Bible verses or devotional materials come to mind?"

"I think of that story from Mary Geegh's book, *God Guides*—the story about the chicken egg."

"I can see why. Thanks. I'll use it."

* * * *

The network meeting opened as usual with lunch and small talk. Cal wanted to ask Curt how he was doing, but he decided to wait to see if it came up after lunch when they would shift to deeper topics.

Devotions came next, and Cal began by reading Lamentations 3:22-23: "Because of the Lord's great love we are not consumed, for his compassions never fail. They are new every morning; great is your faithfulness."

Then he handed out photocopies of the hymn "Great Is Thy Faithfulness" and assigned network members to read the verses and refrain.

Tony read verse one: "Great is Thy faithfulness, O God my Father. There is no shadow of turning with Thee. Thou changest not, Thy compassions, they fail not. As Thou hast been, Thou forever will be."

Rex read the refrain: "Great is Thy faithfulness! Great is Thy faithfulness! Morning by morning new mercies I see. All I have needed Thy hand hath provided. Great is Thy faithfulness, Lord, unto me!

Curt read verse two: "Summer and winter and springtime and harvest; sun, moon, and stars in their courses above; join with all nature in manifold witness to Thy great faithfulness, mercy, and love."

Juan read verse three: "Pardon for sin and a peace that endureth; Thine own dear presence to cheer and to guide; strength for today and bright hope for tomorrow, Blessings all mine, with ten thousand beside!"

Cal read the refrain again and began telling the egg story.

"Mary Geegh was a missionary in India for thirty-eight years, from 1924 to 1968. She experienced many hardships and many times when God showed faithfulness.

"Every morning Mary spent time listening to God for guidance regarding a specific issue she was facing, wrote down what God directed her to do, and then vowed to do it. Many of the stories she wrote about listening to God have been published in a booklet called *God Guides*. I'd like to share one of Mary's stories with you."

Cal turned to a page in the booklet he was holding and began to read:

> I determined to listen to God for guidance in all matters, and I promised Him I would obey whatever He told me. There were so many things which needed solutions. One was a feeling of friction between my colleague and myself. She had ten children and often was not well, and could not carry out her work program regularly. I felt very critical of her for trying to hold onto her job.
>
> One morning early I asked God for guidance: what could I do to dissolve the critical feeling I had in my heart for her? "Take her a fresh egg," came a thought. Well! That wasn't my idea, and who would say that was guidance! A dozen fresh eggs might be reasonable—but one! That might insult my colleague. So, I wrote it off and gave up for that morning.
>
> I went to school to teach my classes in the Mission School. At noon when I came home, there was a chicken in a large armchair in my living room! (Our houses in India were wide open to the public.) The hen flew down and started to cackle and

> there was an egg, freshly laid! Dear me! That had never happened before, nor since. I remembered what I had scratched out in my new "guidance" notebook: "Take her a fresh egg."
>
> "Why not obey?"
>
> "She'll laugh at me."
>
> "Results are not your business. Your business is obedience. You promised."
>
> I took the egg and went to her house. Her little son was outside. That helped. "Here, Tumby, take this egg to your mother, please, it's for her." He took it and went in the house. I didn't wait, but left quickly.
>
> That evening the mother came to me. "How did you happen to bring me that egg? It was so fresh and good."
>
> "Well, that was my guidance this morning." And then I told what happened. "Oh! That's just like God!" she said. "He knew I had nothing to eat this day. There just wasn't enough food for all, so I went without. Then you brought the egg for me. When I ate it, I felt so satisfied and strengthened." From that day she and all her family began to "listen to God" daily for guidance. And all the friction in my heart was gone, and there sprung up an understanding and Christian love for her and for all her family.*

Cal paused for a moment. "When has God given you guidance and then been faithful?" he asked.

He gave the men a few minutes to reflect and then invited them to share their thoughts. Just as Cal had hoped, hearing stories of God's love, guidance, and faithfulness brought a real sense of God's presence with them.

Cal brought devotions to a close by asking everyone to join him in singing "Great Is Thy Faithfulness." They stood and sang out loud

* *God Guides*, by Mary Geegh, pp. 2-3. Copyright 2004, Samuel and Lois Geegh and Marcy (Geegh) Zastrow. Used with permission.

and strong. A few of the people walking by on their way to one of the church's programs paused in the hallway outside to listen then hurried on when they had finished singing.

"Thanks, Cal," said Tony. "Let's take a seat and spend some time checking in with each other."

Everyone looked toward Curt, assuming he would want to go first again. He smiled and said, "I think it might be best for me to go last so my stuff doesn't dominate the entire meeting. I'm doing okay, and I'm also okay with waiting to give my update."

Rex shared that he had been struggling with his seventeen-year-old son. "He's getting involved with a tough crowd and seems to be rejecting the faith. I know God is faithful, but this is hard, and I sure would appreciate your prayers."

Tony led them in a prayer right then, and after the amens everyone said they would keep praying for Rex and his son.

"On a positive note, I met with the Kids Hope U.S.A. people," Rex continued. "We have agreed to start a Kids Hope ministry at God's Community in the fall when the new school year begins."

Tony asked Rex how he was doing with the grieving he was experiencing last time over the loss of two members of his church.

"A few weeks after our last meeting, I started to feel better about how the memorial services had gone and what a great gift their lives had been," he said. "They lived good lives and deserved to move on to be with Jesus. I realized that I needed to let them go, not for their sakes, but for mine. So I'm doing much better. Thanks for asking."

Juan told the group that his ministry and his family life were going pretty well. "My wife and I are committed to having the family take part in the mission trip to Honduras in the fall, and we're both very excited about it. The kids still aren't sure how they feel about the whole thing."

Cal gave an update on everything that was going on with him and Pam and the 5,000 Plus ministry.

"Cal, Juan, Rex, you've made remarkable progress in defining and beginning to live out your personal calling statements. I can see new energy in your faces and hear it in your voices. Cal, you even look healthier. You look like you're in better physical shape."

"The support and direction I've gotten from this group has made a huge difference in my life," Cal said. "When I got your latest email, Tony, I realized we're almost at the end of the six-month trial period we all committed to for this network. I just want to say, I hope we all decide to continue with these meetings. I need you guys! And thank you, Tony, for getting us all together and for coaching me. God bless you, buddy!"

"Thanks, Cal," said Tony. His voice sounded a little husky. "I hope we continue too. Really, we've all just begun to experience new directions and new vitality in our ministries and our personal lives. And now, with people from our congregations beginning the Living by Design journey, there are bound to be many more reasons to continue to encourage and support each other.

"The potential to realize new and deeper spiritual growth in our congregations and our community is huge. As I've said many times, personal renewal precedes corporate renewal."

Finally it was Curt's turn. For the first time since the network had been meeting, he seemed calm and collected.

"I want to affirm what Cal and Tony just said about the impact of being in this network. I vote for it to continue as well. What I have to tell you about me and Theresa and our congregation couldn't have happened without the support you guys have given me.

"For the time being, Theresa has decided to move in with her sister for a while. This was a decision we made together to give both of us time and space to process what has happened and what needs to happen next.

"Theresa agreed to go to marriage counseling, largely because I was willing to go on my own. She says she doesn't know me any more. I get that. Sometimes I don't feel like I know myself. I want to be a righteous follower of Jesus, but then I realize what I have been doing and the lie I lived.

"If I focus on who God is and how Jesus forgives, I feel like there is hope for me and for our marriage. Theresa and I are scheduled for our next counseling session in a week, and I talk with her on the phone at least once a day—sometimes for just a few minutes, sometimes for an hour or more.

"The consistory isn't sure what to do, so they have given me a two-month leave of absence. They've told the congregation that it's for personal reasons. They have all committed to share nothing more for now. Several of them have said that they want to accept my resignation and find a new pastor. I understand this and have no hard feelings toward them.

"A few others have talked about what might happen if I turn things around with God, with Theresa, and with them. One person even said, 'If this happens, you're going to be a great pastor for somebody. Why not for us?'

"Mostly, I'm just trying to keep my sights on what God wants me do next." Curt paused, and Cal noticed his hands were shaking a little.

"This has brought me closer to God than ever before. It's a hard experience to describe. It's like a combination of fear and freedom.

"If I continue to pursue Jesus, I know I will be okay. And partly that's because I know I have brothers like you. Thank you again for everything that you have done, and for letting me share these things with you.

"I do have a favor I need to ask of one of you," Curt continued. "I need someone to partner with me using software that will allow that person to monitor my web activity. My counselor suggested this. If one of you would be willing to join me in this, it would definitely help me kick this habit, this addiction."

When everyone seemed willing to help, Tony suggested that they all agree to install the software on their computers and hold each other accountable. "Based on the alarming statistics we looked at on pastors' vulnerability to pornography, it's a good idea for all of us to do this."

Cal could tell Curt appreciated their tacit admission that what had happened to him could have happened to any of them. And it was true. Cal wondered, as he had many times, what might have happened with him and Pam if the network hadn't offered him a way out of Flat World.

"Curt, thank you for your willingness to be trusting and open," said Tony. "We all benefit because you are part of this group, and be assured once again that we will be there for you on the difficult road ahead."

Rex stood up and walked over to give Curt a handshake and a quick hug. He led the group in a short prayer, thanking God for being faithful and for giving each of them hope for the future.

When they had finished praying, Tony reminded everyone that at the last meeting he had offered to facilitate a Living by Design retreat with members from their congregations. Everyone but Curt had identified people who wanted to take part. They set possible retreat dates to present to the people who were interested.

"One more important item of business," Tony continued. "As a network, we made a covenant to meet for six months, which means our last meeting would take place next month. Over the next month I want you to think about whether you want to continue or not, and we will make that decision in our next meeting."

"Tony, I don't need a month," said Cal. "I can't imagine not meeting with all of you for at least the next year. I'm ready to sign a new covenant today." Juan, Rex, and Curt all said they agreed.

"That's great, guys," said Tony. "It sure affirms what I believe God has been showing me about the importance of our network.

"Before we leave today, I need your help with something," he continued. "In our network covenant we state that we will focus on transformational learning. We have been using the Living by Design process to do that up until now. Here's what I want you to ask yourself: What would help us keep moving forward in terms of our personal development and growth?"

They all agreed to bring thoughts and suggestions to the next meeting.

Tony asked Curt if he would close with prayer. He kept it short and real. Cal could sense how closely Curt was holding on to God.

Those few words from Revelation came to Cal's mind again: "Behold, I make all things new."

Nothing was impossible for God to recreate, thought Cal. Even Flat World. Even Curt's broken marriage.

What Happened Next?

If you want to find out what has happened in the lives of the network members over the past few years, watch Cal's online video presentation. To access it, visit www.all-things-new.org.

References and Resources

Through Seasons of the Heart, by John Powell; 1987, Thomas Moore Publishing. The excerpts reprinted in this book are from pages 21, 56, and 119.

Fierce Conversations: Achieving Success at Work and in Life, One Conversation at a Time, by Susan Scott, Viking Penguin, 2002.

God Guides, by Mary Geegh
Mary Geegh's booklet on listening prayer, *God Guides*, is widely used as a devotional and study guide. It was reprinted in 2000 by Pray America (www.prayamerica.org). To order *God Guides*, call (517) 374-6116.

Online Appendix

To learn more about resources and programs referenced in this story go to www.all-things-new.org.